BOOK THIRTEEN OF THE RIM CONFEDERACY

Inwards Bound

by Jim Rudnick

RUDNICK PRESS

ISBN-13: 978-1-988144-29-0
Copyright © 2016
Jim Rudnick

RUDNICK PRESS

For my Susan...

The RIM Confederacy: Inwards Bound

"Tempted by the dissolution of the huge empire inwards, Duke Scott and the Baroness and the Caliph join forces to send a ship inwards bound, to find new planets for the expansion of the RIM Confederacy—led by the new captain, Bram Sander. Making a mind-reader a ship's captain means more than one might expect, and Bram has to worry about the issues that arise.

Broken now into smaller Warlord realms, the first thing to do is to find allies and that becomes a major thrust in the RIM Confederacy ships first voyage inwards—and that leads to new allies and antagonists too. One Warlord wants to join the Confederacy and one wants to take it over by force and the chances of that happening are real.

As the new secret mine for Xithricite is found by the Confederacy who now mines the red ore in secret, the Warlord fomenting war sends declarations to the Confederacy ship and Bram must respond. Aided by his own red ship and the Leudies gifts, he foists the Confederacy wishes on the Warlords—and the battles begin..."

A Message to you from the Author...

I just wanted to say thanks so so much for reading Book Thirteen of the RIM Confederacy!

As my Amazon bio says, being a youngster in the 1950's meant that I was a voracious reader in what has been called the Golden Age of Science Fiction. That meant that for me, my heroes were not on the hockey rink or gridiron - but instead in my local Library where at 12 I had a full Adult card (thanks Dad!) and took out more than 5 books a week.

Everyone from Heinlein, Norton, Leiber, Pohl, Anderson, Simak, Asimov, Brackett, Gunn, Van Vogt and more....I fell in love with and eventually owned Ace Doubles of my own. And while I never knew who wrote the Tom Corbett - Space Cadet series, I fell in love with them and they had a place of honor on my own bookcase too!

With that kind of an introduction to Science Fiction, it's no wonder that when I got my writing work done, I turned my own fictional side of my brain to writing same. It's one thing I know how to write - and a totally different matter to release same to the world - something that I've just started to work on....

Suffice it to say my own works are rooted in that Golden Age and it's that era that I'd like to one day be known as a teensy contributor to in some small way...

So once again, thanks for beginning my RIM Confederacy series and wait'll you learn about the alcoholic spaceship captain that is my hero, who fights and beats aliens but not the bottle!

Enjoy and remember, in a series, characters develop and mature not the way we sometimes want...instead, it's like they have a life of their own!

And while you can read the series in any order, I'd highly recommend to start with Pirates, then Sleeper Ship, Prison Planet, Ancient Relics, Hospital Ship, Desert Planet, Ruined Memories, Eons Semester, Trade Wars, Brothers Pride, Honeymoon Bottle, Captured Aliens and Inwards Bound too...and yes, there's more coming soon too!

Prologue ~

He tossed on his bunk and thought about the current state of affairs in his life.

He should have perhaps thought about his station as an ex-Adept Officer in the Barony Navy. Also ex-Barony Navy too. Now he was only a plain lieutenant commander in the Duchy Navy.

He swept a foot and most of a leg from underneath the covers and sighed. He knew he was going to amount to something, but what exactly? His life so far had been—well until the duke came along at least—pretty uneventful.

He had grown up on Eons, and his parents had been Issians but had chosen to be merchants instead of working within the cult, for a reason he'd never understood. He'd asked, he remembered, but that had been met with a shake of the head and silence.

He knew that many, many Issians, millions, in fact, on Eons had little to do with the faith, but he had gravitated toward being a faithful member since grade school when he'd seen vids of what it was like to be in the navy as a spaceman. They had definitely been recruiting vids, but after graduation from high school, he had applied and was accepted at the RIM Confederacy Naval Academy, just outside of Dessau.

He'd realized, too, that upon graduation, he

7

would most likely be asked to swear to the faith that he would be true to Eons first and the navy second. That was what was expected by the inner circle—the ones who ran the faith on Eons. And on the RIM too.

When he graduated from the academy, he had been in the middle of the class as he'd excelled at little, but he had at least passed and had sworn his oath to his faith too.

His first posting was on the RN Marwick as their new Adept Officer under the brand new Captain Tanner Scott. Now he was his friend and mentor, but at the time, he had been scary. Tanner Scott had fought those pirates those long years ago and had done well enough to earn a field promotion from lieutenant to captain, up two whole ranks.

The days of being on the *Marwick* brought mixed emotions to Bram as he rolled over onto his left side and faced the bulkhead just a half an arm's length away.

He shied away from other memories and pushed them back, rather than relive the hurt and pain of death and duty for many. The prison riot and his agreeing to resign from the RIM Navy and join his captain over in the Barony Navy was also something he was not going to relive either.

He sat up, tucked the extra pillow behind his head, and sighed. No sleep truck had even gone by for him to grab onto and slide into, and he kept the thought of Gia away.

He would like to see her, and he knew he could do that, but he resisted. *That would be something to hold out for,* he thought as he scrunched that extra pillow a bit to ease down a little on the bed.

Gym tomorrow in the early part of the morning, he thought and grinned to himself.

I'm getting paunchy and maybe a hundred core crunches will help a bit.

"Hurt a bit, for sure," he said to himself as he closed his eyes once more and tried to find sleep.

CHAPTER ONE

At Helena's pointed request, he looked at a couple of the rooms down on the first floor of the ducal palace before his guest arrived. He'd listened to her for more than ten minutes as she spoke of the need to "be" a duke not just in name but in manner too. She'd taken him to three rooms.

The green one in the colored line of salons, he'd simply hated, and he said, "Too green."

She nodded and led on. Up on the second floor was a large salon with tapestries and sculptures and some kind of floating lines on one wall that changed via a projector on the ceiling.

He shrugged and said, "It's okay, and if the last one isn't better, I'll use it."

She grinned at him and the smile was warm and inviting.

Down the hall quite a bit was the ducal trophy room. "Full of heads and other body parts," she said as she opened the door. "But," she added, "this room reeks of, screams of, testosterone. It's male. It's huge horns and beasts and teeth—all subjugated by man. Any man. Maybe by the duke himself."

He could tell she wanted him to use this room and he nodded to agree. "It will be the trophy room," he said, and she smiled even more brightly and skipped away from him as he came around a standing stuffed Jael.

She shook a finger at him. "You meet with her and you try to get the deal you want—but I don't think it's going to be that hard—you're her RIM fair-haired-boy, Tanner," she said, "and I'll notify the concierge where to bring her."

He sat in one of the over-sized leather wing chairs and crossed his legs. Trying to work out what to wear as a duke had been a chore. He wore uniforms. He'd always worn a uniform. And while there was a uniform that the previous duke had worn, it had too much gold and braid, and there were scrambled eggs on the hat too. And medals. He didn't like medals either.

So he'd asked his concierge for help and had nine full color line drawings in less than a day. He'd forgotten that when Royalty asked for something—

it got done. Immediately. And in spades.

He had liked pieces of only two of the newly styled uniforms, so he had asked that the two outfits to be melded together with some parts from one outfit replacing other parts on the other outfit. What he had ended up with was a very minor styling change with a narrower trouser width that was still able to accommodate his boots. The epaulets were replaced with shoulder straps with the rank insignia. It was a small change but one that Tanner did like. Also, he okayed each and every rank insignia from enlisted through warrant officers all the way up to fleet admiral. He didn't make any real drastic changes—a part of the navy world meant that an eagle meant one thing and one thing only. Captain. It meant that the wearer of the eagle was a captain. He'd held off on those changes for a full week—and then had ordered the changes to take place. It was his duchy and now his navy too.

His own uniform was what Helena called "duke light," and he did admit it was pretty succinct.

White. Narrower legs and his best black boots. No braid or sash or scrambled eggs. Instead, the emblem of the Duchy d'Avigdor, three red planets around a blue sun on a field of white, appeared on his left breast as the uniform badge. He added it to the forearm on the right arm only, and he'd picked through the campaign ribbons and had added a few. He'd only added ones for campaigns that he'd actually taken part in—the prison riot put down, the ancient relic finds, the Memories battle, and even the most recent Praix event too. The ribbons had been made by whoever made them, and he'd had no input on their design. He chose only ribbons that were personal to him so there were few on his chest below the Duchy d'Avigdor emblem.

This was what he wore as his daily uniform. He'd kept the fancier ones with all the braid and such for state dinners and the like, but today, he was in his new Duchy d'Avigdor uniform and that made him happy as he kicked his foot in the air and looked around.

From here, he could see four Jaels. There were nine Tanalorgs, and the big carnivores were the most prized trophy on the RIM. In the corner, he saw the head of an Oved—like the one that had gored the good doctor on his last hunting trip to Anulet. There was another Oved head in the corner, but that one was much bigger than the norm. He wondered how that one was killed, and he realized all he'd need to do was to ask the palace AI for that story, but he resisted.

There was smaller game too. He saw a cat he didn't recognize that must have been six feet long. Another animal—he didn't even know what to call it—hung above a corner from a tree, so he figured it might have been some kind of an ape. "Maybe," he said to himself.

He was about to turn around when there was a gentle knock at the door, and he said, "Enter, please."

From outside, the Baroness strode in, smiled at him, and held out her arms. It would be the first time he had ever touched the woman, but he knew a hug request when he saw one, so he grasped her and hugged. She hugged him back, and he was reminded instantly that she was a beautiful woman.

She was tall with blonde hair that reached down to hang over her shoulders. Her beautiful face had high cheekbones and wide full pouting red lips. Today, her eyes were green. He'd seen them before as blue and brown and even once as pink. But today, her eyes were a green so ripe that he was now sad he didn't pick that green room earlier.

She pulled back from him and smiled, still holding his arms. "The duke d'Avigdor—how nice it is to meet you now on equal grounds," she said as she let go of his arms and retreated to sit opposite him, facing the big wing chair.

Helena had spent almost an hour last night trying to update his knowledge of Royals including who's who and where on the ladder a duke was. It was all a surprise to him; he assumed that a Royal was a Royal and there was no rank among Royals. She schooled him on the ranks from emperor to baron. And she leaned quite a bit on the baron ranking— that it was the lowest of all Royals. If a table of Royals all had dinner, the baron would be the farthest from the king. He'd asked for more details on some and had found out, for instance, that the Doge of Conclusion was another way of saying the Duke of Conclusion. Some languages, she'd pointed out, change the name of the nobles, but that didn't change their ranking.

The Baroness, therefore, was below his rank as a duke, so technically, they were not peers at all—he was her superior.

He smiled and sat too and waved at the concierge who brought in a couple of stewards with tea, coffee, and wine along with some pastries too. He favored those raisin tarts, but he waited to offer same to the Baroness. She grinned at him and seized a raisin tart right away to accompany her tea.

He had the same, and the staff left the room. He smiled once more as he took another small bite of the tart.

"Duke—may I call you Tanner?" she began. "And if so, please call me Krista. This is so nice ..." she said, her voice dropping off. Helena had been correct yet once again, and his smile was broad and wide as he acknowledged the request.

"Krista ... yes, Krista suits you nicely. And I'd be

honored to use our first names—in fact, on a personal note, it is so nice to have you even offer that privilege. I used to be a captain in your navy."

"And I was a pleasure girl before I married the baron. If there is one thing I know—it's that all things change, Tanner," she said as she popped the last bit of the raisin tart into her mouth. She dabbed at the corner of her mouth, picking up a crumb he'd never even seen, and they settled in.

"Nice of you to come to see me here, Krista. And it is nice to be able to host this … this …" and he stopped as the word escaped him.

"One might call this a detente—but that perhaps carries too much weight meaning that we were at odds, maybe this is more of new accord between the Duchy d'Avigdor and the Barony. That's it—an accord. And yes, let's talk. Ideas, Tanner?"

He smiled. She had captured the essence of her trip here to Neen, and as usual, she not only found a way to describe the talks but got to say "go" too!

He sat for a moment to compose his thoughts, and as he did, he was more than conscious of those green eyes peering at him over the top of her teacup as she sipped.

"Krista, I think that I will be totally forthright with you. Honest. Frank. With that as the basis of what I'm about to say," he said as she nodded in agreement, "here's what I've been thinking on since assuming the dukedom ..."

He went on for more than twenty minutes, and later he had trouble remembering exactly what he'd said. But one thing he was sure of was he offered what the Master Adept—both the late one and the new one—had said to him. That he, personally, was the fulcrum upon which the future of the RIM Confederacy seemed to be levered upon. He had no idea why. He had no idea at all, but one thing was for sure. He had been front and center of most of the changes here in the past eleven years. He now knew that this might mean more than ever before, especially if he could be proactive—rather than reactive.

The Baroness nodded and nodded often as he spoke and did not interrupt him.

"So, here's what I'm thinking. The RIM Confederacy has about one hundred planets in our forty realms. And it's my belief that inside the boundary buoys, there is little left to explore and bring to the Council as full new members."

She nodded again and filled her own cup of tea from the pot.

He accepted the pot, did the same, and looked at her with as much sincerity as he could muster. "So, what I propose is a linking of three of the real powers here on the RIM—equal partners, that is— and send out a force to go beyond our boundary

buoys to see what we can find. We'd push out into
Pentyaan space, judging by the latest news from
that area. Twenty-three realms all now in turmoil,
and it's my belief that there might be new members,
even. Or new planets for our own realms."

He sat back and sipped, eying the remaining
raisin tart but instead reached for a Garnuthian
lemon tart.

She just stared at him. Moments later, she shook
her head and leaned forward. "Never ever did I
think I'd hear from your lips, Tanner, the desire to,
the need to, grow. New to your realm you may be,
but I think the duchy will be a powerful realm not
only on the RIM but down the arm too," she said as
she reached for the last raisin tart. Nibbling at the
edge, she asked the most important question. "I
take it that as you're asking me—well, the Barony,
actually, you want us to be one of the three realms.
The Barony and the Duchy d'Avigdor—and whom
else?"

He decided to face that with truth so he spoke
plainly. "The Caliphate. I have not yet talked to the
Caliph—but our recent foray over Ghayth was
predicated by his willingness to offer up the
Xithricite ships. He will be in, I think, no problem,
but might I ask—could you accompany me to see
him in person? Any partnership requires honest
and personal touches and—"

"And yes," she said as she chomped down on the remainder of the tart, "so let's go," and she rose right in front of him.

He was surprised by that, laughed right out loud, and waved her to sit back down.

"I see ... I see ..." he said, and his laugh must have been contagious because now she was laughing too.

She leaned forward to touch his hand as it sat on his knee, nodding at him as the laughter lessened. "Tanner. I believed you when you asked if I'd go, and I am so excited by this that I think now—today would be the day. The Caliphate, the Duchy d'Avigdor, and the Barony. Together with more planets than the whole Pentyaan Oligarchy, we can make some real headway. Add in the red ships and those power belts, and what we're talking about is growth, real growth.

That got his laughing stopped cold and he squeezed her hand back. "Krista ... we're not going on a war of conquest—but yes, those will be tools we'll have at our disposal. Of course, I hope to never have to use them; instead, we would be talking the new planets into joining the RIM Confederacy for the other reasons—our longevity vaccine, our Barony Drive, and more ..."

She nodded and let go of his hand, her own now poised over the tray of pastries, and she looked up at him…

"Next time, more of the raisin ones …,if you please, Tanner."

#####

"It's going to be a tough day," he said to himself, but then no one ever told him being a duke was easy. He nodded to Cooper as the *Sword* took its landing port orders from the space station—the *Ensign*—that lay in orbit over Combat, and they began to descend. Helena had helped but the big thank you was going to be for his aide, Lieutenant Commander Kiraz. Her hard work on the research and back story had been most helpful in the late night talks with his wife over the future of the Duchy Naval Academy on Combat.

While there were still several other academies on the RIM, the tide was turning toward the closing of the smaller partisan schools and the movement toward consolidating all navy training to Eons and the official RIM Navy Academy. He'd thought it quite apropos—after all, hadn't he built the damn thing himself, Helena had questioned, her voice light, but he knew that, yes, he'd helped. Their breakup had been responsible for sending him to Eons to be the aide of the admiral charged with the oversight of the new academy towers. And the semester he'd spent there that had gotten them back together too.

But his aide's help, with all the records from the Duchy d'Avigdor archives, including from the treasury as well, spoke more to him than what other realms here on the RIM were doing.

The duke—the late duke rather, had looked at same over the past five years. He had determined, and had even made his decision a written report to himself or to others that might follow, that he would not do as others had done. While he was— and said so in his report—a strong proponent of the teaching of naval skills as a core competency to all students all over the RIM Confederacy, he had a loyalty to Combat—the planet that was the home of the Duchy Naval Academy. A loyalty that had been born, he'd said over the past thousand years that the academy had been in existence, and that meant more to him than the treasury reports.

As the academy was free to any citizen of the Duchy d'Avigdor, the costs were getting more prohibitive than ever. But he didn't care. He wanted the school to survive, and for that loyalty, he'd pay whatever price.

And the last few years, Tanner noted, it had cost even more per student than ever.

And that made him think about what he'd come to Combat today to do—to give notice to the academy headmaster that the school would be closing in one year.

He nodded to Cooper on the great landing, and he followed his aide out of the cockpit seating area, down the main corridor to the landing port and then left once more to the ramp to the ground.

Awaiting him, Ayla had forewarned him, were planetary officials including the president of the Combat Republic. It was Tanner's first visit and one that he knew would be long remembered, but he tried to soften the coming blow with other perks, as Helena had shown him.

He nodded and greeted every single official he met with a big smile, wishing each one well. He nodded to the little girl who presented him with a photo from her elementary school class showing today's festive reception. He nodded and smiled at the president, a youngish man of about thirty, who was eager to show off his planet. Ayla had already nixed about twenty side trips and forays out onto the Combat continents to see this natural wonder or that industrial complex. She had nicely explained that this trip was only to say hello officially, to make a date in person with the president for a full state visit, and then head over to the Duchy Naval Academy.

So he nodded a lot and turned down the kind offers. "Just fitting in a quick trip to ..." he said to another official. He was nice about it and waved them to his aide who took down the particulars.

He smiled more in those first sixty minutes on Combat than he thought possible.

The reception on the landing port pad seemed to go on forever. A couple of times, as the president led him to yet another minister, official, or ambassador of something or to somewhere, he rolled his eyes to Ayla who had to ignore him. But after a full two hours and twenty minutes, or so his PDA said, he was about out of new people to meet.

Ayla stepped forward at his right shoulder. "Your Grace, we will need to leave soon to make our appointment time with the academy headmaster. Pardon for the intrusion, Your Grace."

The president nodded and said, "Yes, yes … we will make that appointment, not a problem." He waved somewhere behind the large group of people around the grouping, and a small motorized bus came roaring up to sit just a dozen feet away.

And, Tanner noticed with a hidden smile, Ayla took charge and wouldn't let any of the group of Combat officials, who stood only feet away, get on that vehicle. She was so good at making them all understand there was no room at all for anyone else, as they had to pick up some academy cadets too, that he chuckled to himself.

Smart choice for an aide … he thought. i

On the bus, she smiled over at him and said,

"Your Grace, we'll make the time with a few minutes to spare. And there are no cadets to pick up on the way either—I made that up to get us out of there, Your Grace." And she smiled even more widely at him.

He grinned back and the ride was now winding along a city throughway at a good clip. He watched as the city went by. He saw parks and high-rise apartment buildings followed by a nest of single-family homes tucked up against a survey of what looked like low-cost housing. They went by a shopping mall that looked like it was from centuries earlier but in what had to be some kind of retro-chic, he thought. "That's a nice touch," he said to himself and asked Ayla to get him some information on that developer as that might be something he might like to steal and use the ideas for new buildings for Neen.

The bus slowed on the exit and took a hard right-hand corner. Ahead of them was the academy. Situated on a large forty-acre plot, the grouping of buildings offered up the full navy experience to all the students. There were buildings that held classrooms, gyms, labs, astronomy theaters, a chapel, stores, the quartermaster, administration, and more. The bus wound up the long driveway and stopped at a nice-looking building with ivy clinging to the walls. White-framed shutters clung to the windows all along the second floor of the building, and the copper roof had long ago gone green with age.

"Your Grace, we're being met here in the headmaster's home here on the grounds. He thought, and I agreed with him, that this would give you more privacy for your talk. I will not be in the study with you two but just outside waiting. PDA me, Your Grace, and I'll come right in," she said.

He nodded. *Should make her a bloody admiral,* he thought as he went up the few steps, and the door opened to allow him to enter. He followed the young cadet down a hallway. The cadet ushered him into the headmaster's study, and the door was closed behind him.

The headmaster rounded the corner of his desk, strode straight up to him, and gave a small smile as he bowed his head. He did not offer his hand, Tanner noticed, but that was normal—one didn't presume to ever touch a Royal. So he smiled back, looked for a chair, and was guided to the one in front of the desk. The headmaster got him settled and then went back to sit behind his desk.

"Your Grace—this is an honor. We have not had a sitting duke here on the academy grounds since, well, since the previous duke's father, Duke Jonathan d'Avigdor more than, what, twenty years ago. So this is both an honor and a privilege, Duke. Can I offer you any refreshments or the like?" he said, one hand playing with a pen on his desk.

The desk was pretty clean. There was a large desk pad with a scene of a graduating class of cadets. There were three picture frames, but he could not see what they held. The IN tray in the top corner to the headmaster's right was interesting. It was jam-packed with sheets of paper. While he could not read the printing on same, he did note some of the papers had bright red boxes printed on them. In his experience, that was the way suppliers drew the reader's attention to the fact that the invoice was unpaid or the payment was late—often months late. While he couldn't ask about same, it was still good to know.

"Headmaster, no thank you for the kind offer of refreshments due to the shortness of our time together today," he said. He did not smile. There was no way to sugarcoat this news, and he got right to it.

"I wanted you to know that there has been a decision made by the Duchy d'Avigdor as to the future of the naval academy here on Combat," he said quietly.

As Tanner caught a breath, he noted the stiffening in the headmaster's back and posture. But he went on.

"It has been decided that we will close this academy, effective at the end of this school year, with our last graduating class. We will move our own students over to attend the newly built RIM Naval Academy on Eons the following semester. I am sorry to have to bring you such news, but I know that you will be a great addition to the RIM Naval Academy. I was able to get every single academy academic position a similar job with the Eons Academy, and you have my word on that," he said and paused for a reaction.

The headmaster neither nodded nor smiled. He took that news in, and it seemed like he was mulling it over, but he said nothing.

So Tanner continued.

"Same deal for all of our students—free tuition, and yes, full room and board at the academy on Eons for free too. Not a dime to become a RIM Navy grad. Expensive, yes ... but we feel that this is the least we can do," he ended and sat waiting.

He didn't wait long.

"Bullshit, Scott ... what you bring is pure cost cutting by the bean counters, and you're a part of that group—some duke you'll be," he snarled and slammed his hand into the desk in front of him, and one of the three pictures fell over. His face was red and he looked like he wanted to punch his duke.

The headmaster's face grew even redder. "More

than a thousand years of heritage and history and dedication to the best navy education anyone would ever get anywhere on the RIM —and it's being tossed away by an ex-drunk who thinks that credits count for more than legacy," he said and he slammed his fist into the desk.

Tanner leaned forward. This he knew how to handle. "If you ever refer to me like that again, I will have you in my brig for a hundred years. I make decisions that are life and death for my men— instead of worrying about a cadet's B-minus grade. You are on notice. We close this place when I said, at the end of this school year. You still have a spot on the RIM Naval Academy academic staff—say one more word, and you'll never work in education anywhere in the RIM Confederacy. We're done," he said, and he stood up so quickly that the chair under him tipped over, but he didn't care.

He walked over to the door, yanked it open, and strode out, surprising his aide who jumped up to try to get ahead of him to open the outer door but failed as he barged right on through. The bus still sat at the front door on the quad around the inner part of the campus, and they got on board.

Tanner waved away any questions for the whole trip back to the landing port, and it was not until they were on board the *Sword* once again as she lifted off under his pilot's skills that he shook his head. He told her what had happened. a

She blanched. "Your Grace ... calling you what he called you, I can't even say it—that's grounds for action—criminal action, as I see it," she said, her voice rife with vengeance.

He nodded but said nothing.

So she waited, and on the trip back to Neen, the *Sword* was quiet.

Tanner had nothing to say. He did know that, yes, he'd just ended the academy, but in his mind, while legacy and history and tradition were all nice, if the Duchy d'Avigdor students were moved over to Eons, they'd get a better education. To compete would cost the Duchy d'Avigdor more than might be gained to update and upgrade everything from labs to equipment, and then there were the huge costs of the academy fleet of ships too that were all past their best too.

"Still, the headmaster had gone way past the pale when he'd attacked me personally," he said to himself. And he'd not been wrong either. He was an ex-drunk. But to say that to a Royal—to your own duke—was something he never thought he'd ever face.

He sat with Ayla on the carrier ride over to the administration building at the Neen naval base, and he still said nothing,

There didn't appear to be anything to say. The

29

decision to close the academy had been made ...

The Master Adept turned and looked at the doorway before her guest even reached the top floor of the tower. She, like all Issians, and better than all too, knew who was coming and why—and more importantly, she knew the results of the conversation too. Being a mind reader was one thing an Issian got used to, but seeing into the future, the immediate future more importantly, was a skill only the best of Issians acquired. "And nurtured," she said to herself, as the acolyte came in to introduce her guest, Bram Sander.

He bowed his head as he walked toward her, and as he drew close enough to almost touch her, he stopped. "Master, I am sorry for the intrusion, and I am sorry for this unexpected interview with you," he said nicely.

She nodded and pointed to the side for him to sit as she did too. The aide had already put a large pot of tea on the table to her left, and she busied herself with pouring tea for him. Being Issian meant she did not have to ask how he'd like it, so he was soon served a new cup of tea with lemon only. As she sat back and sipped on her own, he did as well, and they just looked at each other.

"Bram, you wanted to talk to me—and you will

never be intruding ever. If you'd not 'pulled the pin' as the youngsters say, you would have your place in our Issian inner circle, helping govern the future of our race. But yes, I would like to know why you've come today," she said, sipping her hot tea.

He put down his cup, stood suddenly, and walked over to the large windows that looked out over the wall of the city and the farms below. He swept a hand over all that could be seen and then turned back to face her.

"Master, things here on Eons are changing. Those farms below—I do not know if you've noticed, but some are for sale, and some have actually sold as farmers are coming back to the land. Climate change is with us, Master, and that is a sign of more than new farms. What I mean is, that Eons and in fact the whole RIM Confederacy is now in change. And it's that that I want to discuss with you," he said. He walked back to sit on the beige loveseat and once again picked up his tea.

She nodded. Climate change reports she received monthly, and yes, as he'd noticed too, the blue star of Eons had softened its flow of radiation to the planet. That meant the droughts and climate with season after season of infertile growing was changing. New crops were being planted and harvested, and that was a boon that all Eons citizens were grateful for.

"Your observations are correct, Bram—few others have noted, but yes, climate change is here on Eons."

He nodded. "Ma'am, but there is more. The Praix. Our ex-masters who came here to once again use our Issian skills to aid them in their conquest of yet another galaxy—our own Milky Way Galaxy— were defeated on Ghayth. We hold them now captive on the planet there, and yet that too is an unknown for us—for the RIM, I mean. We need to find the proper way to handle that, Master—we are not slave keepers so the means must be found to help us deal with them. Superior race, perhaps, but it's their technology that is what we should investigate," he said, leaning forward and pointing at her with his teacup.

She nodded and smiled at him. "Exactly what the inner circle discussed just last night in our mind link session, Bram. More than that, we are also going to present a program to deal with the Praix at the next RIM Confederacy Council session as well. I think that your help with that might be a boon to all of us here on the RIM, due to your proximity to the new duke," she said, trying to steer the conversation to an upcoming point.

He tilted his head as he looked at her, and a half smile came over his face.

This one is very much a skilled Issian, she thought.

"Master, yes, I do get your point—but I am not the duke, just a lowly naval officer, nor for that matter, as you know, would I ever look to forward anyone else's future at the expense of his," he said.

She nodded to him and put down her own cup. "But you are in the very unique position—as I've mentioned to you before—of being right at the true nexus of the future of the RIM Confederacy. Your friendship with your mentor, the duke, is a given, but your Issian skills lend to you the ability to help sway and in fact guide at times decisions that will affect us all. All, Bram. All of us here on the RIM are going to be going through changes that make our new farms seem trivial."

She crossed a leg under her robe and leaned toward him. "Plus what I can see in your own future, perhaps you have as yet to focus on. You will be a captain in the duke's navy within a fortnight. You will take a new venture on behalf of the RIM—or the real powers back here—inwards bound, and from what we, the inner circle can see, you will succeed. Oh, there will be repercussions and, yes, regrets, but that is as it will be," she said.

He had a shocked look on his face. "Captain—I'm a captain soon?"

She nodded and replied, "Yes, Bram, I too know that there has never been a navy captain who is an

Adept Officer as well. The why of that I do not know—but you will be the first," she said.

He still looked a bit surprised, so she decided that now was the time.

"As well, we also see that you will be an important link between the Praix and the RIM, but that will not unfold for a while, Bram. And I also need to ask—might you, even in your 'resigned' state, consider being involved in our inner circle mind links—at your own convenience?"

He looked away for a moment out the windows, to where the horizon lay to the east and the now not so bright sunshine. It looked like he was considering that, and then as she saw him make his decision, she acted surprised moments later.

"Yes, I will take part in mind links with the inner circle—if nothing else, I can ask for counsel myself," he said.

She nodded. "Yes, yes, indeed and offer the circle the opportunity to learn more from the captain right on the scene, so to speak," she said.

Niceties were made over the next half hour as they talked about the RIM and some of the issues facing it. He did agree to coming to the next RIM Confederacy Council meeting, if the duke would allow it, to consider the Praix. The only thing, she noted, he did not want to talk about at all was Gia Scott—and that did not surprise her very much.

The Court Martial trial room was just about empty, with the few guests in the visitors area beyond the bar standing quietly as the trial began. The three military judges, Admiral Vennamo and two captains who had long service, were ushered in, and all stood as they took their seats. As the admiral smacked the judge's desk with her gavel, all were asked to sit. The room was a simple meeting room in the Barony Navy landing port administration building, as there was no permanent court martial trial room. The fact was, there had been so very few court martials that this was almost unprecedented.

On one side of the room sat the jury—six officers in the Barony Navy. The four captains and two lieutenant commanders had the job today to weigh the evidence and find the defendant guilty or innocent. Captain Magnusson faced the group of his peers from the table across the room. Beside him sat his defense counsel—a captain in the Barony Navy. He was not a ship's captain, but he was a lawyer with the Judge Advocate General's Corps. At another table, facing the judges, sat the prosecutor—again a captain. "Not one used to being on a ship. Another lawyer," Magnusson said to himself.

"Our world is populated with lawyers who've probably never even been on a ship—and yet these are the people who are in charge of my future." He shook his head and leaned back to listen to the trial clerk who was about to read off the charges.

"Your Honor, on the day in question, off the planet Ghayth, in low orbit, the defendant did commit certain acts, and he is hereby charged with the offense of attempted murder of a Praix alien on board their ship, the *Wisp*. It was an action carried out only by the defendant, and charges are hereby leveled at him according to the Barony Navy Code, section 15-T," the clerk said and sat.

The words attempted murder lay out there for all to think about for a few seconds.

The admiral said, "Thank you, Clerk." He looked at the defense counsel captain and said, "Do we have a plea?"

Magnusson and his lawyer rose. "Yes, Your Honor, the defendant has a plea," his lawyer said.

"Not guilty, Your Honor," Magnusson said loudly and forcefully. He really wasn't guilty. He knew that.

The judge looked over at the clerk and said, "Record that plea, please, Clerk," and he nodded to the prosecution desk.

The head prosecutor rose to make his opening speech. "It was one part of the whole 'gestalt' of that encounter on the landing deck of the *Wisp*. The first contact with the Praix was at a standstill—no violence had been threatened or had occurred. And for no reason at all, Captain Magnusson had taken it upon himself to fire on one of the Praix aliens, wounding him badly. But the alien had lived. The action by the captain had been seen by all present—it had been vid taped and that evidence will be presented later.

"But, there was no threat to any RIM Confederacy citizen when the captain had shot the Praix alien. I repeat, Your Honors, no threat to any RIM Confederacy citizen. None at all; therefore, this was not naval action but, in fact, attempted murder." He sat then and said to the judges, "The prosecution is ready to present evidence to prove this crime, Your Honors."

But before the prosecution presented its evidence, the defense would get to present its opening statement, and just a day ago, Magnusson and his lawyer had argued about that. But Magnusson had been adamant—the truth was what he wanted to present and that was all.

The defense lawyer rose and spoke slowly and succinctly. "May it please the court, we hereby waive any disagreements with all of the items just mentioned in the prosecutor's opening statement, and we stipulate it as true and correct. That is not the issue that we will predicate our defense upon. Instead, as we will show, the defendant was not of his right mind when the actions occurred. We will present the captain himself to offer up what happened in what might be called 'extenuating circumstances' and, in doing so, show that the defendant is innocent." He sat.

The room was silent for a moment, and then the admiral spoke.

"Then let's get to it, shall we? Clerk, please record in the trial logs that evidence that the prosecution will tender to you forthwith— videotapes as well," he said. The prosecution tendered the documents to the clerk up at her desk, and the paper evidence was properly logged in.

Then, under instruction of the clerk, the video tape was played.

It showed the simple record of what happened on the *Wisp*, starting with the group of the five Praix, who were standing in front of Major Stal. One stepped forward a few steps and then fell as he was shot by Captain Magnusson who had run into the camera frame, shouting "Got him, Stal." And then all hell broke loose.

The admiral waved at the clerk and the tape stopped and then faded to black on the big screen that sat on the wall opposite the jury bench.

"Stipulated as factual, defense?" Admiral

Vennamo asked.

"Yes, Your Honor," replied Magnusson's lawyer.

"Then the prosecution rests, Your Honor," the prosecutor said, and he sat down at his desk.

"The defense calls Captain Mel Magnusson to the stand," his lawyer said.

Magnusson got up to take the short walk to the witness box to the left of the judge's bench. He sat and noted the chair was a hard metal one with no padding on the seat. *Probably*, he thought, *to make a witness uncomfortable. Just like me.*

"Captain Magnusson, we have just seen the video evidence—evidence that you insisted on stipulating as true and correct, and in it, you are seen shooting the Praix alien. Can you give us new evidence—not on the act—but on why this event happened?"

Magnusson looked down at his interlaced hands that were perched on the wooden edge of the witness box in front of him. He looked up and then over to the jury—the group of peers who would have his future in their hands—and began to speak.

"I am a good captain—been the best that I can be for my crew and as the most recent captain of the Barony frigate the *BN Exeter* for over a year. I was, however, seconded by the Baroness herself to take on the new task of being captain of the *BN Defiant*

—the large shuttle that was recently refitted with the Xithricite red metal plates. That made the ship pretty much invulnerable to all space weapons, and that is why she was fitted thusly, and we were sent to Ghayth to take part in the final mission with the Praix."

He undid his interlaced fingers since they were almost bloodless, as he'd been squeezing them so tightly. He rubbed them along his thighs behind the wooden front of the witness box and smiled at the jury. The jury stared at him with blank faces.

Magnusson took a deep breath and continued. "This final mission was simply to make first contact. That is what I believe, and that is what I was told. The fact that the *Defiant* carried two fully armed squads of marines under Major Stal is a part of the explanation—as it let me know, too, that should there be any kind of violence, that we—the Barony Navy—could respond. Add to that, that the marines were all wearing these new power belts— ones that made the wearer almost invulnerable to any kind of attack under certain conditions—made that knowledge that we were ready for anything that much more heightened in my mind. In all minds, I'd think, on that landing deck."

His lawyer nodded and said, "Then why did you fire that shot, Captain—when each of the marines were so much better prepared, better armed, and wearing those power belts?"

Magnusson nodded and held out his hands, palms up in supplication. "And that's what I mean too. Why would I ever have done such a thing? The simple truth is—that I did not do this. Someone or something or some greater power made me do that act—one that I had no intention of ever doing," he said as he concentrated on looking into every single set of eyes on the jury.

The prosecutor shook his head and sighed.

One of the judges had a look of disbelief on his face.

A couple of the jurors shook their heads.

"And I mean that. I am a trained professional captain with more than a decade and a half of service here in the Barony Navy. I know what I know—and I know that this was an action—yes, carried out by me but not of my doing in this case. Someone made me do this. Someone who wanted the Praix to react in a certain way—someone, I would think, who could know what the outcome would be of this kind of act ..." he said, and then he was quiet.

No one present for the court martial being held in this room could have drawn any other conclusion but one as to whom Magnusson was blaming for this action. The Issians. Magnusson believed Issian intervention was the only explanation for his

41

actions.

It was now common knowledge that the Praix had come to the RIM to reclaim the Issians, who had been subservient to them in the past. The Praix had also intended to conquer this galaxy and had known the Issians would be required to help—and the Praix had wanted to start with the RIM.

No one witnessing the court martial proceedings had any doubts about what the Praix had intended to do or that the Issians often intervened, but could that have been the case here was the question.

Magnusson's lawyer had only one more question. "What about that event—specifically at the time you pulled that trigger—was the most troubling for you in retrospect?"

"That the weapon that I used to shoot the Praix was a Colt revolver, firing projectile bullets. But I do not own such a weapon—have always used a needler as my sidearm—and there is more than a decade of that history to check upon. In fact, as I've learned since the event, that Colt has also 'gone missing.' That is, it is not in the prosecution's list of evidence either," he said.

After that statement, the prosecution scurried through some of the documents on their desk, and eventually the chief prosecutor looked up at Admiral Vennamo and shook his head … there was no such weapon in the evidence kit.

The lawyer smiled at Magnusson, said, "Your witness," and then sat down.

Suddenly, the rear doors to the court martial trial room opened, and in a rush, the Master Adept appeared along with a couple of aides. They walked right up to stand at the bar before the three judges.

"We ask that we be granted standing here, Your Honors, and will present evidence of our own at the proper time, if it please the court?" she said.

The three judges conferred, and Admiral Vennamo spoke to the court. "We will allow the Master Adept to add evidence—but only should it be needed in our minds. We will reserve judgment of that until the proper time as well," she said. Vennamo was calm, but everyone could see this unusual interruption had rattled the three judges.

The Master Adept sat in the front row, just a few feet behind the bar, and as they got settled, the admiral nodded to the head prosecutor to begin.

It's grilling time, Magnusson thought, and he braced himself for the worst.

The prosecution missed not a single chance to bear down on the "excuse," as he called it, that the defendant was using to try to evade a guilty verdict. He went back to the meeting with the Baroness, and while he skirted the subject of the questions the leader of the Barony had actually asked Magnusson and her desires, he did try to show that Magnusson was more than pleased with the change from the *Exeter* to the *Defiant*.

The prosecutor stated Magnusson was thrilled he was now going to be right at the helm of the action on the Praix. He insinuated Magnusson had seen this as an opportunity to further his career, but then he learned Major Stal, with the marines under him, was in charge.

Realizing he would not be in charge, he'd been more than upset, the prosecutor claimed and explained to the jury that Magnusson had taken it upon himself to attack that Praix alien in the hopes that the action would show the value he would bring to the mission.

The prosecutor used examples from Magnusson's past in an attempt to prove he wasn't a good captain. He pounded away on the defendant's earlier foray in un-asked-for Barony Drive testing via his unauthorized trip to Branton. That test drive was not only unauthorized but dangerous too.

"This is the kind of captain he was—unwilling to wait until proper channels okayed his actions. In fact, that's exactly what kind of a captain you still are, is it not, Captain Magnusson? One who steams off in his own direction with no regards as to outcome. Just like the attempted murder of the

Praix on board their own ship ..."

Before Magnusson could even answer, the Master Adept rose to interrupt.

Admiral Vennamo once again raised her gavel to find the interruption out of order, but it remained raised at her shoulder height—and did not move down. The look on her face was one of both horror and wonder as the whole courtroom could see her trying to bang the gavel down onto the desk in front of her.

She took her eyes off the suspended gavel and then looked down at the Master Adept who stood once again at the bar, staring at her. "This is your doing, yes?" Vennamo said, her voice tremulous.

The Master Adept nodded and then made a second tiny nod with her head, and the gavel now slammed down onto the desk with a crack that was loud and noisy.

"I wanted you—and everyone attending this court martial—to see that Issians can, yes, to a small degree, control some actions by some citizens. I wanted to do that—but I ask for forgiveness from the court in that I used one of the three judges to show what we can do if needed. But in this case— the case of attempted murder by Captain Magnusson—we, yes, were the ones.

"I was the one who sent the captain off to fire that one shot. I ensured that it would not be a fatal shot, but at the same time, I needed to provoke the Praix into reacting as they always do. With violence. With no respect for life. With the single thought that they are the race that will always be at the top of the food chain, as the youngsters put it," she said nicely, looking at both the jury and then the judges too.

The Master Adept continued before anyone could speak. "Which brings me to the point— Captain Magnusson was, yes, controlled by us to do that action, resulting in the Praix showing themselves for what they are. He is innocent of these charges. And before any lay blame at his feet for any of this—remember the gavel? We could have chosen anyone, and it was simply easier to use him. He was on the *Defiant* and he is a terrible shot with a projectile weapon. So we used him," she said, and then she sat down once more.

The courtroom was abuzz—jury members talked among themselves, the prosecution team had their heads together and whispered to each other, and the judges looked to be in an intense conversation. Only Magnusson sat silently, and he stared at the Master Adept over his shoulder.

After almost a full five minutes, Admiral Vennamo banged the gavel once more. "Order, please … order. We have made a decision concerning this court martial matter. We find the defendant, Captain Magnusson, not guilty, and we hereby enter a finding of a res judicata judgment. There will be no further action and we hereby bar any continued or further litigation of this case," she said, smacking the gavel yet again.

Admiral Vennamo turned to address the jury. "Jury members, we thank you for your efforts here today, and you are excused." The gavel struck the desk again.

Looking at the defendant, Admiral Vennamo said, "Captain Magnusson, having been found not guilty, you are hereby discharged and will return to full rank and privileges of a Barony Navy captain as of today. Case dismissed." Her gavel banged one more time.

As Magnusson turned and got up to go past the bar and out into the guest area, he saw only the back of the Master Adept's robe as she left the room.

"Oh, we will talk," he said to himself. "One day, we will talk …"

CHAPTER TWO

On the space station in high orbit over Neria, the Ramat guard snapped to attention so firmly that Tanner thought the alien might have injured his foot as it stamped down on the deck. The ringing from the heel of the guard's boot echoed around the end of the corridor.

Tanner acknowledged the guard with a smile and said. "Duke d'Avigdor to see the Caliph."

The guard moved to his left and pressed the access plate button that he'd been standing in front of, and the pocket door slid in noiselessly. Tanner entered the small conference room and he whistled to himself as the view presented itself out the exterior bulkhead view-port.

The Nerian station was the home of the RIM-wide Vac Jump Championships. That event was coming up in a few days. Around the Nerian Station were docked and moored ships from many of the RIM Confederacy worlds. There were DenKoss water ships, Leudi cargo freighters, and choir ships from Randi docked beside hunting ships from the Duchy d'Avigdor realm planet Anulet. Four or five Barony of Neres cruisers sat out at the fringe of the gathering ships, all docked and supported by gantries.

Chandler tenders were busy ferrying out supplies, and repair droids were blinking their notice lights as they swarmed out to the various maintenance tickets they were programmed to service. Lying at high orbit, the station was a mass of modular wings and units and had been pieced together over the last fifty years in the belief that what happened here on the station would never happen below on the world that owned it.

On his way into the conference room, while braced by four of his own Duchy Provost guards, he'd been bumped and jostled by people who thronged throughout the walkways, the malls, and corridors. Some people almost fought for prime viewing stations at various window ports and scene-scapes that overlooked the almost totally surrounded arena area where the competition would occur.

It was a festive air with everyone excited, and

sometimes, loud conversations over preferred choices of entrants peaked while still others flaunted their own champions. Vacjumpers were well known throughout the RIM, and each colony, duchy, barony, caliphate, and world had its own champions. And in two days, they would meet here on Nerian Station to compete for the annual RIM-wide VacJump Games.

He shook his head at the remembrance of same from more than ten years ago. He'd been assigned then, as the captain of the RIM Navy cruiser the *RN Marwick*, to be the liaison and officer and provide the liaison ship for the event on behalf of the RIM Navy. He'd thought at the time it was just a press or public relations type of mission and hadn't really thought it important. Sure enough, as he remembered now, it had been a bit interesting to see various realm citizens jump out into space with no breathing apparatus or warming suits to see how long they could last before quitting.

He couldn't remember now who had won the big open championship, but he knew the fellow who came in second well. A few years later, that alien had broken into the secure labs on the Barony Hospital Ship to steal—or try to steal—the Ikarian vaccine. He'd made it all the way out to the end of the labs and had, because of his Vacjump skills learned here on the Nerian Station, jumped out into space. Unfortunately for him, Tanner had been waiting and had forced the alien to give up the stolen vaccine. He had died, Tanner remembered, but he had been charged by the Baroness to defend the secure labs and protect the vaccine at any and all costs, and he had done just that.

On his left thigh, without even realizing it, his palm had begun gently tapping there with a "one, two ... one, two" beat. As he became aware of what was happening, he mentally thanked Doctor Etter for helping Tanner to manage his PTSD via the EMDR treatment.

He shuddered for a moment, wondering why he felt this way and realized it was perhaps because he was back once more at a location where something of magnitude in his own future had occurred. Maybe. Maybe it was that. Or maybe he was just struck that it was here he first met someone he'd had to kill.

"No matter," he said to himself as he watched a Roor Navy frigate slowly make some space beside it to allow a smaller sphere ship from Alex'n to moor beside it.

He grinned, wondering how the hell the space station crew could put up with all the requests for space and docking and mooring and even barging together to try to accommodate the huge crowds due here the day after tomorrow. Watching out there along the areas bounded off by marker buoys was fun, and while he could have spent more time doing just that, he turned away from the view and sat.

Time to go to work. Time to try to swing the Caliph over from a new friend—well, maybe an old acquaintance —into a full partner.

He had practiced his presentation with Helena just last night, and she, like him, had pronounced it a good pitch. It would allow the Caliph to be proactive, be aggressive, and be a full partner. Yet, underlying all that, it also allowed him to veer off the partnership too—at least on the surface it looked like that. What might happen, no one really knew, and as he mulled that over, the door to the conference room slipped open.

"Duke d'Avigdor—so nice to hear from you, and I'm glad to have the time to sit and chat with you," the Caliph said.

Today, he wore—once again—the same earth tones of brown and darker brown, and his boots were a shade of brown Tanner had never seen before—sort of a light brown and blue meld. At six feet six inches tall, the Caliph was one imposing alien head of state—there was no doubt about that —he had a hawkish face with brown skin and large nose. He held himself in such a way that it meant one thing to all who saw him—he was in charge, and there was no doubt about that.

He clapped his hands, and from a side door in the forward bulkhead, some stewards wheeled in a full cart of refreshments holding some hot appetizers.

"I think you humans call this a 'tapas' type of light refreshment," Sharia said, and he half-bowed his head.

Tanner grinned at him.

"Tapas indeed, Sharia—and what a pleasant surprise. I was thinking about what might be available down on the station food court area that I could grab before setting off on the *Sword* back to the Duchy—but this is an admirable treat!" he said, and he meant it too.

Like the Caliph, he too dug in and filled most of his plate with selections that he thought looked good, and he grabbed a big bottle of water to help wash the lunch down. They sat and talked about the Vacjump games and some of the recent winners. The Caliph said, "This year, there are more than thirty thousand expected to be here at the games. On the station, on their ships, on the viewing barges"—he shook his head—"the competition is still the biggest draw on the RIM, and all are here to watch the entrants cheat death.

As the meal was ending, Tanner chose to begin his presentation. "Caliph—Sharia, I mean. I wanted to talk to you about the future of the RIM Confederacy," he said as his opening statement, making it about all the realms, not just their own.

Sharia nodded, licked a finger as he slid his plate to one side, and drank some of his juice drink. "What is it you think should be done?" he asked plainly.

So, plainly it will be, Tanner thought.

"Sharia—there are exactly three realms that run —control—look after—the whole of the Confederacy—at least that's how I see it. The Barony, the Caliphate, and the Duchy. The Duchy is the smallest, so we are the ones who might stand to gain most, and I wanted to say that right out front. But what I propose is a partnership between our three realms to expand," he said.

Now wait, Helena had drummed into him. Tanner recalled Helena's advice: Stop the selling, and let him noodle that around. Do not speak next … he must buy in, and if he does, he'll answer you. Tanner followed Helena's advice and didn't say another word. He sat quietly and waited for the Caliph's response.

The Caliph rose, went to the big view-port, and looked out at the dozens of ships that lay around the station. He took another big swallow of the juice and nodded—to whom or to what Tanner had no idea, and he returned in less than a minute to sit back down.

"Agreed. But what exactly is it you propose?" he inquired. His face gave nothing away, and Tanner was once again glad to have never played poker with the alien.

Tanner half-smiled. "What I think we need to do, is to join forces. To send off one ship on what we'd call a 'joint venture exploration' of an area that might be rife with rebellion and therefore have planets that might consider allying with any of us," he said, and again he paused.

"Pentyaan space—you're talking about the recent news of the rebellions on some of their realm worlds and the split up of their whole oligarchy— right?" the Caliph asked, his head tilted to one side.

He was right, of course. Word was that some planets within the oligarchy of twenty-three planets had already rebelled, spun off by warlords to form their own new empires. As well, word had come back that even when attacked by the Pentyaan Oligarchy Navy, they had successfully fought off their old masters.

"Right," Tanner said, "that's exactly what I mean. We would like to take one of your Crimson ships—so that we'd be invulnerable to one and all— and approach them and see what we can see. Make trade agreements, if nothing else, but also offer what a new planet to one of our own realms receives, like protection, and what that would mean to them. We don't know how this might go—and yes, there is some degree of trust needed between us, the joint venture partners. But more than that, with Pentyaan space lying tight to the RIM Confederacy, it'd just be moving some boundary buoys that cement our ownership of all who'd want to join the Confederacy," he finished off. And once again, he waited.

The Caliph nodded but so imperceptibly, Tanner almost didn't notice. He knew the unconscious use of head movements one made often showed how the person was leaning. Alien or human ... those traits were noticeable and the nods or shakes often proved true.

The Caliph finished his juice and then recapped the bottle, twisting the lid so tight that it squeaked. He leaned back, as though thinking, and then leaned forward. "I think that your idea is sound. I like it and will grant the partnership use of, say, *Crimson I* on one condition. That we all agree on the captain—you, me, and the Baroness too. That way, we will all be represented," he said.

Tanner started. That topic hadn't come up in his earlier discussions, and he wanted that captaincy for himself; after all, hadn't he come up with the plan?

"That position I was hoping to fill myself," he

said, figuring that frankness might work.

The Caliph shook his head. "Not possible—you are a duke. If the head of state shows up, any warlord will know what the intent is—and we'd end up fighting our way out of their space. No, it needs to be someone who knows what's expected and can handle anything that comes along. But someone that will represent all three of our realms," he said and sat back, toying with his empty juice bottle.

Tanner was stumped.

Who? Who could I trust—that the Baroness and the Caliph would trust too? Who could be both a captain and a RIM Confederacy ambassador at the same time? Who might, he thought, and then it hit him.

"Then I propose Lieutenant Commander Bram Sander for the new captaincy of the *Crimson I*," he said.

Bram had never been a captain, but he had done time on many navy ships as an Adept Officer. Bram was an Issian—so he had that mind reading skill-set —even though he had retired from their cult. Bram had been in the RIM Navy, the Baronial Navy and now in the Duchy Navy, so he knew naval protocols. Bram could also be counted on to be morally upright and loyal.

He would do nicely, Tanner thought

"Agreed. Good choice. He will be captain and represent our joint venture exploration. He will allow us to expand as I think that is exactly what will happen. And he has those Issian skills to stay ahead of any warlord at the same time. I like your choice, Tanner ..." he said, and he smiled broadly at him.

Tanner nodded back and the talk went back to the Vacjump games, as the lunch meeting was about over.

"Do right by the partnership, Duke," the Caliph said.

Tanner nodded. He intended to do just that for all three of them.

Gia sat on the chair looking out the big windows again. *Facing south maybe,* she thought, *but it makes no difference. Don't think it will ever change.* The scene was the same today as it had been yesterday. There were some schmaltzy-looking gardens stretching out for about a hundred yards below, and then the tall wall that surrounded the ducal palace grounds. After the wall was the open park that lay around the whole area, and eventually toward the horizon, she could see the edge of Neen City. From here, she well knew after being cooped up here for twenty days now, the view was the same. *Day after day,* she thought and grimaced as she realized the view would always be the same.

One year in six rooms. One was her bedroom, which she had to admit was nicely furnished with all the furniture and art being antiques she thought. Thick, thick carpet ran the full length of the large bedroom, and the ceiling was coved and had built-in lights and fans too.

The bathroom had just about every single kind of hygiene appliance there was—at least in her world. There was the usual toilet and bath and a full-size shower. *Could fit at least a dozen people,* she thought. There were two bidets with some buttons in the bathroom. *That's odd,* Gia thought, *wonder what they'd clean.*

Gia paid particular attention to the bathroom as she was used to a simpler setup. There were two hot tub Jacuzzis in the enormous bathroom. One Jacuzzi sat inside and had special venting that kept any kind of odor away. The other Jacuzzi was outside on a wide and long balcony that loomed out over the gardens below. *One would have been enough. Don't know why I'd need two.*

Rounding out the bathroom was a full massage area, complete with a call button that would bring the masseuse directly to her suite of rooms. On her first trip into the bathroom, she'd seen a card on the pillow that listed the various types of massages, treatments, and every kind of waxing one could imagine. She had shuddered when she read that

she could ask for toe hair removal, and she
wondered who might need such a thing, but she'd
have that conversation with herself on a slower day.

"Like any day was not slow," she said to herself
as she twisted the glass of cider in her hands. She
could have asked for anything including any
cocktail she could think of, wine, beer, liqueurs, or
spirits too. But the cider that had been
recommended was nice. *Very apple-y tasting, but
nice,* she thought.

She had other rooms though. There was the
official salon, where she had been told all meetings
with the court officers would occur. She thought the
room was a hodgepodge of an old-fashioned palette
of colors compared to the new very minimalist
furniture. She didn't like that room, but that was
probably the kind of reaction that was wanted with
the room. Saved for official use only, which was
what it was intended for, she thought.

The room she called her living room was a
smaller room with a couple of seating areas. She
really liked the seating area with matching couches
facing each other in front of the real log-burning
fireplace. She could toss some pillows against one
end and then stretch out on the couch as she
requested a vid or streaming media to be displayed
on the big screen that sat above the fireplace. She'd
already done that quite a few times, and she knew

she'd have to slow down on that or else it too would become boring, and over a year, that could happen all too soon.

She also had a private study, as the court officers had called it. They had brought her to the palace and escorted her into her own wing, which they told her had been set up specifically for her use. "My captivity is more like it," she said to herself, and yet, somehow and somewhere deep inside her, she knew it was a fair sentence.

The three judges had taken more than two weeks to make their decision, and she'd been sent back to the courtroom to hear her verdict and sentence too. The head judge had droned on, she thought, for far too long on the terms of compos mentis and the mitigating circumstances of delusional thinking. He'd then gone on to say that while the decision on the bench was a split decision, the defendant was found not guilty due to those delusional symptoms and that the sentence would be one full year of house arrest in the ducal palace.

That had been about twenty days ago, and she'd been transferred first by bus and then by Jeep to the rear of the palace where she had been marched inside in handcuffs. She was escorted up to the third floor, to the end of the main corridor, and then down a short hallway to a locked door.

The court officers had told her the locked door

was the only entrance to her wing, and there was no way to reach that entrance except via a corridor off the servants quarters. She had also learned her wing had been built more than one hundred years earlier, but it had been refurbished just a few decades ago. That was decades of non-use trumped by what might have been an apartment that had had six different designers work on the rooms. But she didn't care. This would be home for another eleven months and a few days.

She had not even been in the sixth room yet. It was her meeting room. The court officers had told her this was the only room where she could see other people. She could invite guests and they would be escorted to that room. Once inside, there would be a court bailiff posted on picket duty to prevent any security concerns. After the visit, the bailiff would then escort the guest directly out of the wing and then lock Gia back into her wing.

This she felt was beyond the pale. She could not understand why she could not have guests—any guests in any number—in any of her rooms. She'd already asked her lawyer to appeal, and that process had just started.

In the meantime, she sat, like now, and did nothing.

Well, not nothing. She was going to wait until the dinner hour and then ask the AI for something hard to find and cook. She had spent more than an hour in the living room using the Gallipedia hook-up to find local food recipes for Neen, and it had been an easy thing to do. She had found one, and she was ready to challenge the AI.

This is what I've become—a person who solely looks for hard-to-make recipes for the palace AI. She shook her head and quaffed down the end of the glass of cider

"I will find something to spend my time on," and as she said that to herself, she thought of her brother, but she threw out that thought quickly.

There would be no thinking of Tanner. Not until he came to see her in person—she had no position on him at present.

She did wonder about her mother once again, but she pushed that aside too. The doctor had said she suffered from a delusional state due to her mother.

She knew now that the Tribunal was right and Tanner was innocent of the death of her sister Nora. But her mother had said no, the Tribunal was wrong. She had kicked Tanner out of the house as soon as the Tribunal had ruled. She had said over and over that Tanner was the reason why her favorite daughter had died. That had grated on Gia's nerves for years.

She shrugged and said, "AI, more cider, please, but five degrees C colder."

Moments later, she heard a beep from the wall unit where these things appeared. She got up, went over, and slid the door open to retrieve her colder cider. And it was colder, and she liked that. The fact that AI was probably recording her every move in her apartment she could ignore, but not being able to get a cider at the right temperature was inexcusable.

Soon, it would be time to ask for that dinner, and while she was sad to say it, it was the highlight of her day.

#####

Trade Master Lofton bowed his head as he entered the small gym and was now in the presence of the duke. He had walked over from the doorway to stand in front of the Royal, and as was customary, he bowed.

"Not needed, Trade Master Lofton, friends do not need to lean on state protocols. Welcome, Niels," the duke said, and a breath punctuated every single word. The duke was working on a rowing machine, and rivers of perspiration ran down his temples and coated his shoulders. While it looked like he was tuckered out, Niels made no assumptions. This was a man, he knew, who was very hard to read.

"Duke, thank you for the EYES ONLY and the

chance to speak to you," he said.

The duke nodded and continued to row, row, row as he stared not at his guest but at the display monitor on the rowing machine in front of him. "Wait just a minute please ..." he said, and he suddenly increased his rowing speed. Pushing quicker now with his legs and his large forearms bulging as he pulled on the machine's oars, he counted out loud. "One, two, three ..."

After getting to what must have been his goal of one hundred, he slowed and then pulled a foot from the push rod stirrups, and the whole machine slowed down. He nodded to his guest, and as Niels watched, he stood and grabbed a towel from a stack of pure white gym items and waved the trader over to the side. He sat heavily onto a bench and pointed to the one across from him as he toweled off the sweat from his head and arms. Dropping the towel into his lap, he reached for the water in the big bottle on the bench and smiled at the Leudie.

"Please excuse my few minutes there, Niels—had to finish my routine," he said as he chugged down the water in big gulps.

"Not a problem at all, Duke d'Avigdor," Niels answered.

"I need to ask you something—so I thought it better asked in person, and it concerns, yes, the power belts that you so kindly donated to the recent

mission over Ghayth," the duke said. He looked
directly at his guest and a small smile now
appeared on his face. "I wish to know if we can re-
borrow those belts—well, actually, I'd like to know
how many you have and whether or not I can once
again borrow them?" he asked.

Niels leaned back and took that in. It was an
unusual request but one that he could speak to.
Being a full member of the Leudie Trading Rules
Group, he was one of the top thirty traders on his
planet who made the rules for the rest of their
traders—the whole Leudie economy, in fact. The
belts had come to them after they'd sent a trader
ship inward more than three thousand lights, and
the trader had found them and brought them back.
But they'd only been able to get sixty of the belts—
at least at this stage. There had been some
grumbling about that, and he knew this would be
addressed at the next meeting; there would be a
vote to send a ship powered by the Barony Drive to
the same system to see if more of the belts could be
obtained. But right now, there were only sixty.

"Might I ask, before I answer, Duke, why you
might need them? Lending them to help defeat the
aliens was one thing, but surely there are no more
threats here on the RIM, are there?" he asked. As a
trader, Niels needed more information before
giving an answer. Gaining information was one of

the tenets of any successful trade, and this was no different.

"Yes, surely. I am mounting a mission—of exploration mostly—into Pentyaan space. We will send one ship—the *Crimson I*, so you know that the Caliph is a partner on this too as well as the Baroness. That ship will be exploring—looking into the rumors of the breakup of the oligarchy and how that might be good for the RIM Confederacy. Should there be any kind of issue with some of the planets we visit, we'd just like to have belts on our marines. Not in any way for aggressive force—but to supply invulnerable defense is all we're after. Might that work for the Leudie realm?"

Niels thought on that, and seeing an advantage, he smiled back at the duke. "Duke, it also comes to me that there may be some kind of new planet gathering—into whichever RIM Confederacy realm, as a part of our own realms. That would mean that there would be brand new trading opportunities. So yes, while we have thirty belts available, I can offer that we would, again, lend them to the Duchy d'Avigdor for this mission, on the proviso that should any new trading opportunities arise—that Leudie be granted exclusive access to those planets. For, say, a period of ten years. Would that work for you and your mission?" he asked.

He'd held back thirty belts, and he'd also asked for exclusive rights for ten years. That would make the Leudie Trading Rules Group a group of happy campers. Nothing could destroy the belts, so he risked nothing, really. So instead of sitting on a shelf somewhere on Leudie, the belts would be out helping to gain new markets for the Leudie traders.

The duke's head tilted to one side, as he thought about that offer. And then he nodded. "Done. That's an offer that I find more than acceptable, so yes, we will proceed based on that," he said, and he smiled at Niels as he once again toweled off his arms.

Niels smiled. "We will send them to?" he asked.

"Just here to the duchy navy yards, attention please to CWO Hartford. He'll get them all shipshape and will sign the manifest no problems at all, Trade Master," the duke said as he rose. He tossed the towel over one shoulder and smiled once more. "I thank you, Niels, for the quick grasp of the situation and how we both—the Duchy d'Avigdor and Leudie—might turn this exploration into a real opportunity for us both," he said.

Niels nodded back. "Add in your own 'luck gene,' as we Leudies call it, and I think that we— the whole RIM Confederacy—is in for new opportunities, Your Grace."

The duke shook his head. "I've no idea about this

'luck gene,' Niels, but I do know that our mission is going to be successful—aided by you and your belts. So thank you," he added, and he clasped Niels by the shoulder and patted his shoulder a couple of times.

On the way out, led by a Provost guard, Niels smiled to himself. A good deal had been reached—ten years of exclusive trading on any new worlds that came into the RIM Confederacy. He well knew that was something any trader would be proud of.

#####

The silver eagles lay in their box, now open on the table in front of Bram, and he just stared at them. Silver eagles with their wings spread—the insignia of a captain in any man's navy. He had just opened—been ordered to open—the box by the duke who sat and was still grinning at him. Seated in the duke's office in the administration building, they had been talking now for more than one hour.

Tanner had been explaining what his next big mission was to be—the joint venture partnership between the Caliphate, the Barony, and the Duchy d'Avigdor. He had taken quite a while to show why this had to be the RIM's next big move—at least why he thought so. He also took the time to explain the various partners he could have chosen—and why he'd picked those two. He shared how the partners had contributed too—the *Crimson I* and the *Defiant* were their buy-ins.

Bram had asked many questions and had drilled down on some things that Tanner as yet hadn't even decided. Whose navy regs would the *Crimson I* be under? What were the rules of engagement should there be conflict? More questions followed and Tanner just waved them off by saying those would all be decided by the captain—the new captain.

He had laid a box in front of Bram on the table and directed him to open it.

The silver eagles shone brightly in the fluorescent lighting in the room. Bram put the box down and raised an eyebrow. He stared at the eagles for a moment and then seemed to need to wait for a moment.

So Tanner waited and didn't say anything.

A couple of minutes later, Bram nodded. "I take it you mean me?" he said, his voice a bit incredulous.

Tanner raised an eyebrow and leaned forward.

"Me? I'm well below a captain's rank, Your Grace. This is … this is—"

Tanner interrupted him quickly. "This is a field promotion, Captain Sander. You're as of now a full Duchy Navy captain, and your first captaincy will be on the *Crimson I*. You will lead us into Pentyaan space to see what we can see. You are the captain, and you will report to me and me alone—I will look after our partners—and the admiral too. There is one small catch—not a deal breaker at least how I look at it. And, there is a hidden advantage too. Your XO will be Daika Rostrum—the Roma refugee—and that comes as a part of the Baroness's buy-in," Tanner said.

Bram nodded. He knew her, of course, since he had spent time—both on and off a ship—with the refugees. "But wasn't Daika a captain?" he asked.

Tanner nodded. "Yes, and that's not the real hidden advantage, but still a positive one. You get an XO who's sat in your chair before—a bonus for sure. But the real advantage is that Daika is just back from a month of being in Pentyaan space. She was involved in Xithricite mining and exploration, and she knows that space; after all, the Roma have been trading and scavenging throughout the Pentyaan space now for years."

Tanner stopped selling and waited.

Bram reached for the eagles and grinned at his mentor. "Your Grace—thank you so much for this opportunity, I will not let you down. Do we as yet have a date for the start of the mission?" he asked, his grip tight on the box of eagles.

Tanner grinned at him. "You're the captain, assemble your crew and ships and resources right here—this will now be your office in our administration building. You're good to go when you decide it's time. You're the captain," Tanner said, and he dipped his head to his protege.

Bram nodded and leaned forward to offer up his hand. Tanner reached out, grabbed it, and shook it heartily. He knew Bram would be a great captain.

And no matter what the Pentyaan space threw at him, he'd more than succeed.

CHAPTER THREE

The *Crimson I* was what the navy called the
"stretch" model of frigates, and at almost four
hundred feet long, she could carry one hundred
forty-five crew members and twenty-nine officers.
For this mission, however, the new captain had
decided to go light on personnel, and she carried
only ninety crew members and fifteen officers. That
had given him room to house the thirty marines in
their own crew section with some small degree of
comfort and privacy. Otherwise, as he'd learned
when he'd talked to Major Stal before they made
the final plans, the marines usually had to camp out
in one of the two cargo bays, but that wasn't an
option this time. The *Defiant*, the Barony Xithricite
shuttle, was carried in the landing bay, and to make
room for her, the walls had been pushed out, which

meant both cargo bays were now gone.

The major had grinned at Bram when they'd been planning the shipboard changes. "We can just hang on to some ropes maybe and that'd work—hey, we're marines and used to second-class treatment, right?" That had gotten a laugh from all at the meeting. The *Crimson I*'s XO, Daika, had smiled and shared that she'd run into something like that years ago and five hundred lights away, and that story had sent the meeting off on a tangent.

But it had been decided. The cargo bays were to be made into a wider and higher space to house the aft end of the *Defiant*, as she was more than fifty feet too wide for the landing bay.

"That'll get her in okay, and when we exit, it's a straight out only," the ship's science officer, Harvey Walton, had said dryly.

Bram hadn't thought it would be a problem, and they had gone on to other items.

Later in his ready room, once the meeting had broken up, he pulled up the view out on the landing port at the Neen naval yards on his console. As he had expected, there was still a lot of equipment and techies swarming around the ship. He had looked out over the yard and had seen two Alex'n sphere ships, a Leudie trader, an Alto freighter, and four Duchy d'Avigdor Navy ships too.

"All getting ready to go somewhere for something," he had said to himself.

The work on the ship had been completed in nine days. Probably, Bram had figured, because his requests for speed from the naval yard crews had been emphasized by the duke himself. The crew had been assembled, and Bram had happily met Major Stal and had squared him away himself in the officer quarters area, having reserved him a private bunk for some degree of privacy.

His XO though had caused him some degree of discomfort at first. Daika was, or at least had been, a captain all on her own. Now, she had been demoted—not by him but by the Barony Navy—to the rank of commander. One step below the rank of captain, but surely that would smart, he thought. As he had sat and talked to her for the first time, in this same ready room, he had tried to feel her out about that demotion. His major concern was if it would play any part in how she handled the mission the *Crimson I* was going out on. But for all intents and purposes, plus as she probably knew, Bram could take a look inside her head at what lay behind the words she spoke.

After a quick peek in her mind, Bram discovered she was looking forward to a successful mission. She believed that if the ship found new worlds that might join the Barony, then the Barony Navy

would need to grow. And that would mean that
experienced navy commanders, like her, would be
made into new captains on new ships. Bram had
thought ambition was important to her, and he had
made sure to note that in his own personal ship's
log.

Earlier this morning, the *Crimson I* had lifted off
Neen, and using the Barony Drive, it had jumped
to the edge of RIM space. As the *Crimson I* passed
by the RIM Confederacy boundary buoy, the helm
announced same to the bridge and Bram in the
ready room.

They were now in Pentyaan space, and the
Crimson I had left home for the unknown. Bram
checked his star charts himself, having blown up
the chart onto the view-screen now, and he looked
at the real estate in front of him. The helm was
aimed at the big trading planet of Oirus, about five
lights away and one he'd never been on before. But
as his XO had filled him in on same, he felt this
would be a suitable spot to start their mission.

They had visited it often, she'd told him, but it
had been more than five years since her last visit.
Still, it was a wide-open trading planet, and the
Crimson I would be no different a visitor than any
other.

He killed the star chart and left his ready room to
take the captain's chair. "A damn fine thing to be

able to do," he said to himself yet again.

Sitting in the captain's chair, he looked up at the bridge view-screen and noted the blue planet below. With no space station, they had to await the Oirus landing port notifications. As he looked around, he saw there were three other ships in low orbit.

"Guess there's a queue?" he said to his helm officer.

"Roger that," Lieutenant Shelia McCray answered, "and we wait, Sir."

He didn't know much of the bridge crew yet when it came to their foibles and personalities, but he knew right off the bat when he'd interviewed for bridge crew that McCray was the one. A tall girl at almost six feet in height, she seemed to have forgone all the items that made a woman a woman. She had a bald skull—shaved or depilated daily, he suspected, as it was so shiny. She wore no makeup at all. Her eyebrows were bushy yet they did suit her look. Big wide earrings swung from her earlobes, and each finger had a ring. A woman for sure, he noted, that couldn't hide her great figure yet seemed to not care a whit. She would be all business, Bram had thought from the first moment they'd chatted, and he had hired her on the spot.

While he watched the view-screen, the flashing icon that came up from Oirus appeared on the sidebar.

The bridge Ansible officer, Lieutenant Peter Brush listened to the message in his ear buds and then half-turned to speak to the captain.

"Sir, just granted landing pad number nineteen —and we can go down at will, Sir," he said. Bram thought his Ansible officer was a nice young man. He was five years out of the Duchy Naval Academy over on Combat and had great performance reviews, which had sold Bram on this crewman too.

"Roger that," Bram said. "Lieutenant McCray, take us down."

As the ship slowly yawed to port and InertialDrive took her down, the view-screen display bar kept up with their movement as they went down to their assigned pad.

"Science—what can you tell us about this planet?" Bram asked over his shoulder.

Lieutenant Harvey Walton grinned. "In twenty-five words or less, not much, Captain. But here's the basics. Been a part of Pentyaan Oligarchy space for over three hundred years. Global population of almost three million. Big industries are mining and manufacturing—but we're talking medium-grade tech here. Nothing that we don't have already out on the RIM. Trading center is in the capital called Crisus, and that's just adjacent to the landing port below. Should be a real hodgepodge of ships already landed, as this, I'm getting from Gallipedia, is the planet's big trading holiday. Well, it's ten days long ,and this is only day three, Captain ..." he said.

Bram nodded and then thanked the crewman. *Big trading holiday, eh?* he thought. *Seems like we can use that to chat with others as well as planetary citizens too.*

He watched, as the whole bridge crew did, as the clouds came up at them and then parted eventually to show the city that lay off to starboard. There was a large curved bay of an ocean farther to the right, and the city occupied the whole end of the wide expanse of water. Bram saw beaches of sand and watercraft out on the sea. As the *Crimson I* dropped farther, the view changed to a coastal mountain range on the north side of the bay running toward the west. The city itself was not so high-tech looking. There were no towers taller than a dozen floors or so, nor were there any real expressways with traffic. Instead, it looked more, Bram thought, like a city that just grew as it grew ... no design or city fathers had worried much about how it looked, he surmised.

"XO, what can you tell us of who's in charge here?"

Daika stood at her bridge station behind him and

spoke out clearly. "Sir, while not having been here in over five years, things have changed, I would think. We've heard that the whole Pentyaan Oligarchy has fractured into four separate and distinct groupings. This one, Oirus, belongs to Warlord Tunander, or so he's called, the Gallipedia entry says—updated, I note, only a month ago. From the original five ruling families, with the loss of one completely which broke up the oligarchy, there are four warlords who now run their own realms. Tunander has four planets, Warlord Genro has three, just adjacent to Tunander. Then there's the big two other warlords, Noriega with six and Konoe with ten planets. Each appears to be a separate realm, with little or no intercourse between them. Very much a change from what we experienced here just half a decade ago."

Bram nodded.

"The only family who had made up the ruling class had all been killed in a huge explosion—their spaceship, it was said, had been destroyed in less than a second. As it had carried the whole family on an outing, there was no one left to rule, and that is what caused the Pentyaan Oligarchy to begin fighting among themselves. And the results were that the four remaining families became warlords in charge of their own realms of planets," Daika finished.

It's this kind of milieu that we find ourselves in, Bram thought. *And this is the kind of semi-vicious change that we might be able to make work for the RIM.*

At least he hoped so, and the *Crimson I* settled down on the ground.

On the landing pad, waiting for the *Crimson I* to land, were Customs and Health officers, like on all worlds, with clipboards in their hands. As the frigate's landing ramp came down off Deck One, the landing party, led by Major Stal, trooped down same.

First, the greetings occurred. Paperwork was handed over for the crew lists, manifests of cargo which were empty, health records for the whole crew, and finally any exemptions and notifications. Normal check-ins, Bram thought, and he was more than impressed with his XO. Daika not only knew what to tender but knew to find a few things to compliment the low-level clerks with. Her promise to tell their bosses later, via her survey report of the landing process, was smiled at warmly.

A little schmaltz works, Bram knew, and he lightly touched the minds of their hosts and saw they were more than pleased with this new visitor to Oirus. Nods and promises of a beer later in the landing port pub were also well received.

As the officials began to move away, one who had been standing at the rear of the group stepped forward and spoke to the XO.

"Ma'am, might I inquire about your purpose in visiting Oirus? I am Sithe Ogrunder who works for the warlord's communication section. I ask as we note that the ship is a RIM Confederacy ship and that you carry no cargo at all ... and I would like to update our files," he asked nicely.

The XO smiled and pointed at Bram. "This is our ship's captain, and he can certainly answer you," she said.

Bram thought about this for a whole second, and then he smiled. "Yes, we're from the RIM Confederacy," he said as he pointed to the ship, "and our Duchy d'Avigdor Navy badge is plain to see."

Up above at the bridge level on the ship, the Duchy d'Avigdor Navy icon of the three red planets around a blue sun on a field of white was brand new and still shiny.

"And yes, this is our first trip into Pentyaan space —"

Sithe Ogrunder held up a hand. "Captain—with all due respect—we no longer refer to the old oligarchy as such—this is now referred to by one and all as the Tunander Coalition. So welcome on behalf of our warlord to the Tunander Coalition," he said.

Bram grunted. If they wanted to call the kingdom

fruit salad, he couldn't care less, but he smiled, nodded, and continued. "Yes, as I was saying, it is our first trip here, and we were hoping to talk to someone with the Oirus government about trade deals or ideas for trade between the RIM and the Tunander Coalition. Who might that be?" he asked. But he thought he knew the answer and he was right.

"So happy to hear that, Captain, and the person you'd want to speak to would be the warlord himself. Might I suggest that I contact the correct departments and try to arrange a meeting—while you and your crew enjoy Crisus over the next few days? I will get back to you soonest on this—I am not trying to delay at all, it's just the huge planet-wide holidays do intrude on new items at times," he said and smiled once more.

Bram watched the personnel carrier move off toward the far line of buildings at the landing port, and he turned to his landing party. "XO, please, let's get the crew some shore leave, and Major, same for your marines too—if you folks like to do that," he said, and the guffaw back from Alver was loud.

"Aye, Sir, will do," both the XO and Alver replied at the same time, and that got another laugh as well.

"So we've days probably before we can meet

with the warlord. XO, tomorrow, I think, I'd like to take a quick trip on the *Defiant* over to see the uh … that previously visited spot of yours. Can that be arranged?" he asked. He wanted to see with his own eyes the moon where the Xithricite mining was still going on.

"And we want that trip to be, what, just a day trip, Sir?" Daika asked.

"Yes," he said, "a nicely quiet day trip is perfect."

They all smiled at that, and as they returned to the ship, Bram was smiling.

We landed, we met the Warlord's clerk, and we're going to get a meeting with him, and tomorrow we will visit the mining on the moon over Birdland … so far so good …

#####

The *Defiant* headed out at dead slow, as the XO herself took the pilot's seat on the Xithricite-clad shuttle. She carefully hovered above the landing pad next to the *Crimson I* and then pointed her up and accelerated the InertialDrive, and the ship climbed steadily up and out of the gravity well that lay around Oirus.

Aboard, Bram and Alver sat up front immediately behind the pilot's seat, and behind them, Alver had added a squad of his marines. All wore the silver power belts and all were armed with the .454 Casulls too.

"Why the old-fashioned firearms with the power belts?" Bram questioned.

"One never knows," Alver said. "Forewarned is forearmed."

Bram sighed. "Too many old saws in one sentence made the import of same less."

"One should never count your chickens until their hatched," Alver said and grinned.

Bram shook his head and chuckled, and the others chuckled too

At the low orbit point, the *Defiant*, under Daika's skilled expertise, yawed well to port. The Barony Drive was engaged and the ship leaped toward the star that was dead ahead. It was the Memories system, only five lights away, and it took less than three seconds to make the trip. Once there, the *Defiant* took a low orbit position and then just sat there.

"How long do you think?" Bram asked his XO who shook her head.

"No idea really, Captain. But let's sit for a full hour, then hit Birdland. That way if the warlord is tracking us somehow, we can just say that we were looking around at empty planets is all. Won't last through much of an investigation, but as an alibi, it should work. Perhaps, that is … depending on how 'trusted' we are ..." she finished off.

He nodded and then laid back his head. *Time to catch some Z's with a quick nap if that is possible ...*

But it wasn't to be. The Ansible squawked at them, and the XO had to talk to the Memories landing pad officer to refuse to touch down at this point. "The *Defiant* is just doing some internal diagnostics. I'll get back to you later if anything changes," Daika said.

He sat up and looked around. The size of the *Defiant* was small—about a hundred and fifty feet long—with most of the space in the rear open for cargo or personnel if needed. He smiled as he recalled the way Alver had packed in the two platoons of marines off Ghayth during the Praix ship attack.

Good to have him along, he thought, and he smiled once more.

Being a ship's captain was, as far as he was learning, more about the thinking of what to do, whom to trust, and what goals one needed to pursue than the ship's battles and actions with others. *Least so far,* he thought...

As the hour chimed up, he grinned at Daika and said, "Birdland's moon, if you please," and he sat back for the ride.

She powered up the InertialDrive and spun the *Defiant* to the left. Pushing the throttle a bit, she moved the ship away from Memories and then engaged the Barony Drive.

The *Defiant* now had a new star in the cross hairs of the bridge view-screen, and in a few seconds, they arrived at what they all called Birdland, a large planet with no sentient creatures at all, it appeared. It was the normal blue, cloud filled, and covered mostly by seas. The duke had told him that at some point a previous duke's wife must have visited Birdland. That duchess had visited Birdland long enough to note the odd yet interesting bird life on same. She'd even imported some for her aviary back on Neen—and while Bram had not seen same, he thought he might like to one day.

But the planet itself was not the real attraction. Instead it was the asteroid field that surrounded the planet and its moon. Some were small in size, but he could see some were big. *Big enough to land a cruiser on, being miles across,* he thought.

Daika punched some coordinates into the helm console, and the *Defiant* went back to InertialDrive and slowly swung into the asteroid field. She carefully threaded the ship around some and over others, and not one seemed to cause the *Defiant* any degree of difficulty. After more than half an hour of this, she spun the shuttle to starboard, and with caution, she approached a big asteroid. This one had a valley that had craters of other previous smaller meteor strikes from eons ago. At one end of the almost flat plain, he could see a ridge of crags jutting up and into the blackness above.

As their ship slowly crossed over the crater plain, the Ansible sounded. Bram nodded to Daika to put it on speaker. "Yes, this is the *BN Defiant*—code 7TTY. We are just looking over the mining situation and will not be landing, so please continue," he replied, quoting the code from his orders.

As his ship moved off the end of that huge crater, below the far lip sat another shuttle, right on the asteroid itself. It too was a Barony Navy ship, and its job was to take a full load of Xithricite ore from the mines, just a few hundred yards away, up and over to Birdland—to land there and move the ore to a Barony frigate, the *BN Callisto.*

As the Defiant moved over the Callisto, the mine itself could now be seen. It lay against an outcrop ridge where the red ore from the tail end of a meteorite had buried itself. The mining crew had erected three scaffoldings around the thirty-foot-wide ore block. One of the mining crew stood up top, and around his waist, he had tied and supported the metal framework of the saw. Below him and off to either side, two more crew were standing, and their jobs were to swing the saw from side to side from the focal point above, held by the man on top. It looked like slow work, and he'd heard it took almost a full two hours to saw off a piece that was about ten feet long and six feet wide. Each slice was only four inches thick, and while cumbersome to manage, the pieces were all carted off by other crew and stored in the shuttle for transport back to the *Callisto* later on.

The XO set the *Defiant* to hover above the mine, and they watched the miners manhandle the huge slab of ore so that it would slide into the shuttle hold. While in space, the ore weighed nothing, but Bram thought that piece alone would weigh ten tons or more on Neres. He smiled.

"XO, I think we've about seen enough. Any numbers as to the amount mined so far from this meteor?"

She checked something on her console that only she could see and smiled. "Not really, but the *Callisto* reports that they've made four full runs back to Neres City—and her cargo limits are four thousand tons, Sir."

Alver whistled. "That'll cover a lot of ships," he said, which got many nods throughout the room. "Maybe we should arrange to make a trip out here, say, once a week? Just to keep tabs on the mining and to look around as they're pretty focused on the asteroid and not so much on the system too. Smart from a military standpoint, XO," Alver said, which got a nod from Daika.

"Back to Memories and then to Oirus, if you please, XO, and put her down right beside the *Crimson I*," Bram said, and he pondered that tonnage. *Will need to figure out what it takes to cloak a ship in Xithricite and divide that ship tonnage into the totals gathered so far ...*

"Captaincy ... always in one's head," he said to himself as he grunted, and *Defiant* jumped toward Memories.

It had taken the admiral what he'd later call too much time, but he had followed the directions—orders may have been a better term—of the chairman, and the Praix captain stood in the executive committee meeting room, awaiting the meeting to start. It had taken some work—and a full squad of RIM Navy marines along as insurance —to go to Ghayth and work out the details with the alien via one of the Issian inner circle. It had taken almost two days—of what the Issian later said were little items—to get the Praix captain to agree.

But yes, he finally agreed he would come along to the executive committee meeting. He would listen to their requests, and if needed, he and the Praix under him would comply. There may be some negotiations, the Praix had added. The Issian had thought that was strange since the word for negotiations was not in the Praix vocabulary.

The Issian had accompanied the Praix here to Navy Hall on Juno, and they'd only just arrived. The admiral sighed. "While the room was more than big enough for the seven usual members, with the much taller Praix now in there too, it felt jammed," the admiral said to himself.

They had set up one of the alien's perch plate sets over against the wall-to-wall bookcases, and the alien stood on the upper plate that sat a foot above the lower plate of the pair. The admiral looked over at the alien and noted that while he could usually see the middle four rows of each column of books and knickknacks, the Praix blotted it all out. The Praix stared at the members of the committee as each came in, and with the late arrival of the chairman, McQueen said to himself, "Guess we're ready to start."

Chairman Gramsci nodded as he looked at the members seated around the table and then took a moment to look over the Praix. *Wonder if the Praix is a guest or a prisoner,* the admiral thought. Beside the alien stood two marines—wearing power belts per the admiral's directions—and each was armed with.454 Casull revolvers. Neither marine looked at anything in the room but the Praix. Beside the alien sat the Issian from the inner circle—Issian apostle

Jana Jelinek—who looked at McQueen and smiled.

All seemed to be all right with Chairman Gramsci, and he nodded back to the admiral.

Don't need to be an Issian to get that pat on the back, McQueen thought and grunted to himself.

He noted the slight smile that appeared on the Master Adept's face and the apostle's face too. "Noted," he said to himself, and he thought for a moment about the weather outside. The first hint of rain hit the windows that looked out the front of Navy Hall as the skies opened up.

"Let's come to order, shall we," Chairman Grasci said as two hands held the Agenda, two more were clasped over his belly, and the last two were busy with a tablet.

"Talk about multitasking," McQueen said to himself, and he smiled at anyone who glanced over at him.

To his left sat the Master Adept, then the Baroness of Neres, and then the Doge of Conclusion, and Chairman Gramsci sat directly opposite him. To his right sat the Duke d'Avigdor, Tanner—a protégé of his in his new role as a Royal —and then the Caliph who was, of course, one of the most changeable Royals on the RIM.

"First order—in fact, wait," the Chairman said, "I'm going to change things up. We'll go over the less important items first to clear the decks for the

Praix issue. First up then is the Tillion female issue. From what we've been able to discover—and by we, I mean the best RIM IT team, our Tarvos experts found this out—the vid that appeared to show the Tillion zygote labs is, yes, really verifiable tape. But the voice-over and the point of view that the Tillions intentionally are not raising females is incorrect. Not true. The truth is, that they do try, but that for some reason—and after generations of testing that is still not finished—the females all do not live. Not a one. To hide that—that shame I might think would be the word—they present to the rest of the RIM Confederacy a point of view that women—their own—will never be seen, which one can see is just hiding the fact that they have none. They also therefore—as we all know, fight any contact with any of our own RIM women too. All of this was way blown up out of proportion and presented in a way that seemed to show that the fault lay with the Duchy d'Avigdor for this." As he said that, the duke stirred and tried to interrupt, but the chairman held up a hand to stop him.

"Which, of course, is not true. So far, our IT team has not yet found out exactly who did this—and yes, we do know already that the suspect vid was not shot by the Barony either. So far, it's an ongoing investigation—but no blame can be assigned as yet to any RIM Confederacy realm," he said and looked around at the members.

No one said a thing, so he nodded and slapped a gavel down on the table lightly. "Carried, and next is the issue of the—"

The Baroness interrupted. "If I might, please, Mister Chairman, may I ask a question—about our guest, please?"

Never knew there were that many shades of white ... if there is any such thing, Admiral McQueen thought as he gave the Baroness his attention and waited to see if Gramsci would allow her to continue. *Perhaps tints might be closer,* he thought, as there were tiny differences between her white boots, leggings, blouse, short jacket, and even the scarf she wore tied into her hair. All were white, yet all were a different color. Trying to figure out what colors the head of the Barony was wearing made the admiral's head hurt, so he gave up.

Gramsci gestured to the Baroness, who nodded and continued. "My question is just to confirm—as we were told before this meeting—that the alien here cannot hear us nor for that matter does it have any idea about what it is we are discussing—correct?"

Her question was on point, McQueen knew, and he'd asked the same question twice today.

"I will pass that question along to the Master Adept—Ma'am?" the chairman said.

The Master Adept smiled at them all and then nodded. "The Praix do have ears, but they are unable to understand what it is we say. They do not have vocal cords, so they do not talk. Over the past few hundreds of thousands of years, their race lost the ability to speak—all because of their superior mental abilities which allowed them to be telepathic. They can use their minds to speak to each other—and to us, the Issians. And that is why they came here to make us, once again, their servant race. We can both use speech to talk to the lesser races, as they call them, and communicate telepathically to them as well—the perfect match. But as you know, we refused to once again be the Praix slave masters, as they called us twenty thousand years ago," she said.

Perhaps it is my own feelings here, but to me, it sounds like is was more than happy that the enslavement of the Issians had not happened, McQueen thought. *True enough.*

"So no, while we talk only using voice, the Praix can hear it, but it is all alien speech to him. It means nothing unless we—either Apostle Jelinek or I—send the gist of what is said here to him. And we are not doing that," she said, and the Issian sitting over beside the Praix against the bookcases nodded.

"Fine, then hopefully that will suffice, Baroness?" the chairman asked, and that got assent from her readily. "Back to the Agenda—one more item, that is, the recent mission—joint mission, I'd like to add, of the Barony, Duchy d'Avigdor, and the Caliphate too—into Pentyaan space. It came to our attention, via the crew interviews held on Neen—um … from the 'also-rans' who spilled the beans, as they say. Seems that the three of you here have some kind of a joint venture happening? May I inquire—on behalf of the RIM Confederacy—officially, what the hell is up?"

The admiral sat up a bit straighter. This was news to him. The three culprits looked at each other, and the Caliph spoke up first.

"We—the Baroness, Duke, and I—decided to send off a ship, our own *Crimson I*, to Pentyaan space to look around. It's a simple exploration mission—with the proviso that should there be any opportunities that might present themselves, the captain would get back to us soonest. And so far, not much has presented itself, so far—but we are hoping—and that's all the news we have on our partnership," he finished off.

The chairman tapped one finger from one of his six hands on the table. Slowly. Over and over, as he was thinking. "You are aware of the rumors of the breakup of the Pentyaan Oligarchy into smaller warlord kingdoms, are you not?"

The duke took this question. "Yes, Chairman,

and our report from the *Crimson I* of last night
confirmed those rumors as being true. Which—as
I'm sure you can agree—is an opportunity for the
RIM Confederacy too. Expansion is always
something that every single member wants, and this
huge space, with its twenty-three realms or warlord
kingdoms, as you put it, might be just what we're
looking for, Chairman," he said.

Today as all days, the duke wore the white
Duchy Navy uniform, and he sat nursing a large
bottle of water. He stared straight at the chairman,
the admiral noted, and that made him smile inside.
The duke was a comer, no doubt about it.

The chairman nodded and then asked one more
question.

"The captain of the *Crimson I* is—"

"Captain Bram Sander of the Royal Duchy
Navy, Chairman," the Baroness interjected.

That took a moment for them to all digest; none
of them missed the fact that the captain was an
Issian. There had never ever been an Issian at that
rank in any RIM Confederacy navy. But not a
word was said.

"Fine," the chairman said. "Now to the Praix
issue. All else we can deal with at our next meeting,
so ... Master Adept, would you care to speak to this
item?" he asked, and he folded four arms over his
chest. One hand still held the tablet while the other

was leafing through a folder in front of him.

She looked around the table, and McQueen tried his hardest to see if he could feel any little tendril of mind linking in his own head, but he could not. He leaned back in his chair, ready to listen to what the Issians had worked out with the Praix. He knew that it might—most likely would—change the future of the RIM Confederacy—but how Was the question.

"We have talked at some length—well, mental talk, that is—with the Praix on Ghayth. Your Commander Williams was a real help for us, Baroness," she said as she looked to her left and smiled at the woman in white, who dipped her head in reply.

"The Praix, as I think most of you know, are, well, housed is the word perhaps, in a brand new hangar on Base-1's landing port on the planet. That gives them some big interior space to fly, which is always a good thing for any avian race. Also, the commander added in full perch facilities that we provided plans for, as well as supplying the Praix with hygiene items, latrines, and even full Praix cooking facilities. Like most birds, they eat, or at least can eat, raw food—and they are omnivores with some items that are very much staples. And again, the commander was a great help in finding sources for same and then providing those foodstuffs on a constant basis. My best regards to that man, Baroness," she said, and she dipped her head in return acknowledgment.

"But the real work was the discussions between the Praix and us trying to decipher their past—well, their current past—and why they chose now to come to the Milky Way. That, we thought, was the crux of the matter, and it was not easy.," the Master Adept said.

"How so?" the Caliph interjected.

She nodded to him and almost shrugged. "Because, that was the one thing that they were most loath to divulge. We got the honest, at least as far as our own ability was able to tell, honest thoughts that they did want to come here. To start in the RIM, on Ghayth, and first, get us back as their slave masters. Then to go through the RIM Confederacy, realm by realm, enslaving us all— some more than others, but we didn't get any kind of a list. But the part that we could not get out of them—for more than a month at least—was why now? What prompted them to leave their SagD galaxy and come here? The captain claimed, as did just about every other Praix, that it was just their own choice. But, and this is usual for all brains when you're looking at forty-some-odd of them, one Praix had a different thought. One of them was worried about suns. Suns going out. Suns turned off by the invaders. All of which meant nothing to us—until we called the captain's bluff."

She half-smiled at the chairman and then went on. "While we had so little information, we pretended to have more. The nice thing about using telepathy between an Issian and a Praix is that one can hide thoughts and information from the other. Easily. Or one can show it."

She turned then to look at the Praix who still was perched back against the bookcases. "So the Apostle Jelinek held that thought—the one about stars that went out as the invaders were responsible for same—in her brain as we talked once more with the captain. He could see that she knew the truth but that I was either unaware, or hiding it. It caused him to, well, to rethink, perhaps, his position, and he came clean, as you humans say. And his story was pretty much the apocalypse for the Praix. The invaders, he said, were simply eradicating anything they found. Everything they found. They moved into a system and dropped some kind of bomb into the system sun. That made the sun go nova and ended all life in the Cinderella zone. It was like," she said, "a black curtain was being dragged across the SagD galaxy, one star at a time."

Admiral McQueen spoke up quickly. "So that means that if they were running from a superior race, survival was the reason they came here. Pretty much running for their lives, I'd say."

That got nods around the table.

The Master Adept nodded too and then turned to look at her Issian Apostle. "Jana, please tell the Praix captain that we now all know of their plight. And that we are searching for an answer to see if we can help. But that such a solution seems to be beyond our own meager skills."

The apostle dipped her head to indicate she would do just that, and she stared up at the tall alien beside her.

It took only moments, it seemed, as the two stared at each other. The Praix did shift his talons a bit on the perch and leaned to one side for a moment. Then the Issian turned away to look back at the Master Adept.

"Ma'am, it thinks that there is no way that such inferior—that was the word he said—species could succeed when the Praix themselves, with fifty millennia of civilization behind them, could not. But he did thank me—well, us—for trying. But he also sent through the thought that when the stars here begin to go out, we will know real fear. At least that's the word I think he meant—fear is not a word in their vocabulary it seems, Ma'am ..."

The Master Adept nodded and thanked her apostle. "Which is what we now know to be true, sad as the news is ..."

The chairman looked out the wet raindrop-covered windows and said nothing, the admiral noted.

The whole committee sat quietly and let that sink in.

"Anyone know how many settled systems the Praix have—or had—in SagD?" the Doge asked.

They all looked at the Master Adept who looked at her apostle who looked at the Praix. She must have asked the Praix that question as moments later she said, "There were more than twenty-nine thousand settled systems in SagD, and the captain says their holdings were normally growing by a few hundred a day. That, and he also added that the Praix had settled more than twenty or so galaxies within more than five million lights from SagD too. From Fornax to the Clouds, they were the top of the food chain—until the invaders came, that is, he added."

The committee members stared at one another as they all thought about those numbers.

"And for these invaders to finish off all of SagD—surely that will take centuries, right?" the Baroness asked.

"At, say, two hundred stars a day—it'd take less than half a year before SagD is dark," the admiral said.

"Of course, there is no way to know how many

novas they're producing per day, but if they put their nose to the grindstone, we've only half a year to come up with a plan."

"A half year," the Doge said, "to save the galaxy? Good grief ... is that what we need to do ..." he asked, the depression in his voice so very noticeable.

"A few things to consider, and yes, Admiral McQueen, your math is correct in that we probably have at least half a year—or maybe centuries. Because, more importantly, what we're missing is that the Praix have already colonized other galaxies —the Milky Way is not the next one. It could be any of the galaxies that the Praix was colonizing over the five million lights their empire extended to."

That seemed to help a bit, but the Doge was still shaking his head. "Oh, we have some real problems —in that the Praix are running from these invaders and they're so far ahead of us that we won't stand a chance. Now that old human saw of 'would the last one leaving turn out the lights' comes to mind," he said as he sounded even more depressed.

"Which is why we broached this idea to the Praix. That we take some of them to the wreck on Ghayth, and they give us its secrets. And their own ship. And the warehouses we've found on the Ghayth arctic and other continents too. We were ably helped in this by the Baroness, and she will allow us access to the whole of Ghayth. And as she has made the promise to share all of the Praix secrets from Ghayth with the RIM Confederacy— we thank her here publicly."

That got some table knocks from the meeting attendants, and even Admiral McQueen smiled and knocked on the table too.

The chairman looked down at his Agenda and sighed. "Okay, we appear to have the Praix issue in hand—now, let's deal with those unimportant ones —trading, economy, and the political unrest over on Olbia. Trading first, and that gets you all this handout ..." he said.

As the meeting clerk went around to hand out the thick document about some kind of trading issues, the admiral took in what had just happened and thought, *Either we have six months 'til we face these invaders or hundreds of years ... I know which one I'd like to face ...*

At the edge of the landing port, where the gate led out into the city of Crisus, Bram and his party were met with what could only be called a show of strength. Ahead of them in what Bram thought looked like a truck sat twenty armed guards. The cab of the truck was tall enough to hold another guard, standing up, who had his hands on some kind of an automatic weapon. It was not pointed at the RIM group, but it looked like it was on a gimbal that could swing the gun to bear on them in a second. Behind it sat an empty carrier, which Bram assumed would be for them. The driver of the carrier ignored everything going on around him.

While Bram was looking at that, the door opened on the small shack that sat beside the bar across the roadway, and out marched Sithe Ogrunder, the Crisus citizen who worked for the warlord. He was smiling and that was a good sign.

"Belts on," Alver said, and they all reached for the small switch behind their silver power belt buckles. Once that switch was pressed, they were totally protected from everything but the .454 Casull projectile weapon. Bram followed suit, remembering that on the ground—any ground—the major was the man in charge of security for the mission.

No one noticed anything with the belts, which was fine. Their protection would probably never even be tested—or so they all hoped.

The communications section warlord, Ogrunder, waved them around the bar across the road. They were soon ensconced in the now full little bus-like vehicle, and the lead truck with the guards moved away. Following closely behind, their driver kept a short distance between the two, and there really was no way to look ahead. Instead, they watched to each side, seated two by two with Bram beside Daika, Alver beside Lieutenant Walton, their science point man, and then the four marines. Each wore the power belt and each was carrying the .454 Casull sidearm—a nine-shot automatic—with two clips each on the holster sides.

I feel armed and dangerous, Bram thought. *I feel like I am the king of the hill.* And then he grinned to himself. *This is all the belt talking ...* The feeling of being invulnerable was one he'd never ever had to be conscious of, and he did like it.

As the vehicle drove on, the city of Crisus went by on their left and right. Ahead, the machine gun guard was holding on to the side bars around the turret he was in, and over his head, one could see just the top of a few buildings that eventually flowed by their vehicles on the left or right.

The buildings appeared to be newer with what Bram could see looked like a bustling commerce in and around them. There were sidewalk cafés, office towers, and restaurants. A few small parks held buskers and tables with what looked like arts and crafts items. No one, Bram thought, would be willing to spend the time and effort to sit in a park trying to sell homemade jewelry or crafts if there wasn't anyone who wanted to buy same. Years ago, Bram had learned this was one of the easiest ways to see if a community was vibrant and growing.

Crisus was alive. So that meant that, at least at first thought, the population was happy with the status quo.

Not a good thing then for my mission to find new realms for the RIM, Bram thought, *but still good for trade possibilities for the duke et al.*

He sighed, but then he remembered this was the first of the twenty-three worlds in the Pentyaan system, which was now known as Warlord space. Perhaps other opportunities would come by, and he shrugged since he knew it would all unfold in the near future.

He sent a quick tendril of a mind link out to Warlord Ogrunder. It wasn't enough to let him know that he was being scanned by an Issian brain, but it was enough to see what the man was thinking.

"Great that we took the main way to the warlord's buildings" was the thought that was on the surface. Below it was a sense of dread that Bram could not see any clearer at this distance or in these circumstances. A busy ride in an open vehicle, with much other input, made anyone's brain too unfocused for him to get a real read. *Maybe later,* he thought, just as the big carrier ahead of them moved

off to the right-hand side of the street and turned, and their driver followed.

They passed through an arched driveway in a solid wide and long building. The stone used to build the structure was a shade of gray with a bit of rusty red mixed in with it. The two vehicles went through that portal which was about thirty feet wide. Inside the archway, there was a courtyard, which must have been a hundred yards square. The building had three stories and a multitude of windows looking down at the wide cobblestone courtyard. The carrier with the guards and the turret gunner pulled off to one side, but their driver instead drove straight across the cobblestones and stopped at what looked like a reception committee.

Everyone who had accompanied Bram emptied out of the carrier and turned to follow him over to the group in front of the large staircase going up and into the building.

Bram stopped a few feet short and looked at them all; there were about a dozen of them in what looked like a stage production usher's uniform. Large epaulettes jutted out six inches from their shoulders. The military style hat had a big swoop on the top and more scrambled eggs on the brow than he'd ever seen before. Facing forward in the center was a circle in blue that held three smaller rings of a salmon color, and in the middle was a diamond that was coal black. Bram guessed that icon represented the Warlord's Coalition, but its design and colors meant little to Bram.

I'm glad the duke doesn't have us wearing uniforms this gaudy, Bram thought. *These folks like more like courtiers than military men.* Bram's eyes widened as he took in the rest of the uniform, which was even gaudier. The pants were extremely wide at the knee and then tightened to tuck into the salmon-colored boots. Covering the chest on the left side, the shirt had row after row of ribbons with medals below the ribbons too. *Lots of medals, more on this group of warlord acolytes than one would find in the whole marine forces in the Barony,* Bram thought.

He ignored all of that as the short man in the front of the group stepped forward.

"Welcome, RIM Confederacy citizens, to the Warlord Coalition here on Oirus," the man said and threw a salute.

Bram snapped back one in return.

"The warlord awaits, please follow me," he said, and he turned on his heel and went up the stairs quickly.

The group from the RIM went next, and they were followed by the rest of the well-uniformed courtiers.

They went through a large triple doorway, then straight ahead over a beautifully marbled floor in grays and whites, then down a long corridor to a big door on the right. Their guide simply opened up the door and then stood to the side.

As Bram walked through the doorway, he realized he was in a very formal presentation room. The long narrow carpet ahead led to a set of ten stairs and up to a dais where a man—the warlord, he assumed—was already seated. On either side stood people Bram thought might be the warlord's advisers or counselors. He ignored them, walked the whole way down the long carpet, and then stopped at the bottom of the stairs.

"May I present, Warlord, the RIM Confederacy captain of the *Crimson I*, Captain Bram Sander," a voice from the group to one side of the warlord called out.

Bram nodded and then mere seconds later, he bowed Deeply and then stood.

"We recognize the captain and offer our warm greetings to the RIM as well. So good of you to visit, Captain. What can I offer you—refreshments perhaps?" he asked.

Bram kept a straight face as he took in the warlord's appearance. *So many gold leaves on that hat. Looks like the biggest pile of scrambled eggs I've ever seen surrounding that icon badge.* He wore the same uniform as the members of the group who had met them at the building's entrance, but the warlord wore a sash in bright red of some kind of shiny satin fabric. On it was that same icon badge and some stripes that must mean something to others but meant nothing to Bram.

Bram smiled and said, "No thank you, Warlord Tunander, we are all fine. Instead, might I make a request that over the next few days, we sit and discuss new trading opportunities for the Warlord Coalition and the RIM?" he said pleasantly.

As he was talking, he sent out that little tendril of a mind link to see what he might find on the warlord's mind. And he found, unexpectedly, that the warlord was interested in one thing and one thing only.

Revenue for his coalition.

The warlord was interested in incoming revenue that would help him balance his small budget. Bram received that image quite clearly, and he knew he should have guessed that up front. A new realm with few trade deals and probably all in the red meant that the man in the big chair needed to build his treasury.

The warlord smiled at him. "We think that will be a wonderful way to see if there might be ways for each of us to profit from new trade opportunities," he said, and he motioned to one of his advisers on one side.

A man crept up, leaned over to listen to the

warlord, and made some comments back. And then he stepped back.

"With the big holiday upon us, we have some state functions we cannot move nor change, so the closest time we can have those talks is two days from now. In the meantime, we will take you on a short tour of the coalition—you will visit each of our worlds besides Oirus and then we meet. It will give you and yours some extra information about us and our worlds, and in that way, perhaps, we can have a widely based new trade pact," he said.

On the face of it, Bram thought, *that does make sense.* He nodded and agreed, and in less than a minute, the RIM group was out of the building and onto the same small vehicle to return to the Crisus landing port.

As they rode along, still behind the turreted carrier of guards, he wondered if that had gone as it should have. *So far, everything was as it seemed,* Bram thought.

So far, there are no little clinkers on the horizon like my grandfather used to say—even though this is an "absurdistan" type kingdom, but my grandfather would then add at least not yet ... guess I better be prepared.

CHAPTER FOUR

It was not at all surprising to Bram to see that the faces looking at him all still had eyebrows that were arched up as high as they would go. Five members of the coalition group were in front of him on the landing pad at the bottom of the *Crimson I* ramp. He'd gone down same to meet with the group who were going to be taking his party on the tour to all the other coalition planets, and he'd made all ten of those eyebrows arch up with one sentence.

"Well, yes," he had said as he considered the offer to go over to one of the coalition ships, "but if we go in our ship, we can make the whole tour in a few hours."

All the eyebrows had lifted, and the five members just stood there and looked at each other.

The leader of the coalition group, their usual

113

escort, Sithe Ogrunder, had smiled halfway and then asked, "How might that be possible? The tour, as I've already said, is the full size of the coalition and that is approximately twelve light years across."

He was careful, Bram noted, to not make any kind of a statement that Bram might have just exaggerated or even lied. Bram smiled at the man and took the job of explaining the new Barony Drive to the group, and those eyebrows stayed up. "Come aboard, and you'll see—we'll be on this first one on your list," he said as he held up the tour itinerary sheet he'd just been given by Ogrunder, "in less than five minutes. And yes, the Barony Drive—available to any and all RIM Confederacy member realms—might also be a part of any trade deal with the RIM too," he said, knowing that would be a major card to play.

Minutes later, they were all ensconced in the seats behind the cockpit of the *Defiant*, and at Bram's command, Daika, his XO, took her up and out. Getting the coordinates to Ventos Prime, the first planet to visit today, took a moment, and then she nodded over her shoulder to the captain.

"And we're off ..." Bram said and the Ventos sun, in the cross hairs of the view-screen, suddenly jumped, and in six seconds, there was a chime, and the *Defiant* popped out of sub-space.

"Sir," Daika said, "this is um ... Ventos Prime, I believe it's called," she said.

The sputtering and looks of incredulity from their guests was well worth the showing off, Bram thought and nodded back to her. "Very good, XO, please take us down when we're okayed by the landing authority," he replied.

Beside him in their seats, the coalition guests were taking notes, and one was recording the bridge view-screen including, he noted, the sidebar that said their time of flight was six seconds.

When it comes to cards to play, the duke will have a really good hand with the Barony Drive in the pot, Bram thought and grinned.

The authorizations came almost immediately, and the *Defiant* went down on a slow long glide to port. After gliding down a few hundred miles from high orbit, a normal-looking planet lay beneath them. Blue oceans, brown and green continents, and banks and banks of clouds filled the view-screen. A ring of islands was easy to see too, and Bram wondered if they might be like Bottle—the RIM Confederacy planet that had just joined the Barony yet was still everyone's first pick of a planet to vacation on.

As they moved a few more miles down, the cities below could be seen, and one of the coalition members shared that the planet's capital, Lazar, was the big city on the ocean's coast where the landing port was located. The landing port was surprisingly huge. Many ships were already down, and it was no real surprise to see what they were doing—loading up some kind of liquid cargo.

"Oil is what Ventos is rich in, and it is a real moneymaker for the Tunander Coalition. These ships trade our refined petroleum—gas, diesel, petro-chemicals, propane, and all the plastics too— and ship it to our trading partners. We do quite well on Ventos." Ogrunder smiled as he boasted about the first stop on the tour.

After putting the *Defiant* down and then getting the confirmation from the landing authority, Daika spun in her chair and said, "We're okay, Captain. Shut her down?"

Bram thought on that for a moment and then held up a hand to hold that conversation.

"Can you tell me, Ogrunder, what exactly this tour entails? We'd just like to learn about the planet, and you can't do that sitting on a landing pad in the capital. Nor for that matter by meeting officials and smiling ..."

The coalition group leader nodded back to him and spread out his hands. "Captain, this was not my doing—but yes, there are probably twenty or thirty planetary officials who wish to meet you and tell you what a great planet Ventos is—and that was by the warlord's doing, Captain."

His hands were tied, but Bram decided right
there and then that he was the captain and it was
his ship. "So, let's be Defiant," he said to himself.

"Sorry, but we don't have the time or the interest
for that kind of diplomacy. Pilot, let the landing
authority know that we're going to take an aerial
tour first. Then time allowing, we'll come back.
Daika, take her up soonest," he said.

She spun back around in her chair, made some
console moves, and moments later, the *Defiant*
Inertial Drive lifted the ship up. At about a
thousand feet, she spun the ship to move inland and
away from the ocean. She took her up in a long
slow rise, and in a few more miles, the *Defiant* was
at ten thousand feet and moving over the landscape
just below.

The first thing they noticed was the huge tri-level
pipelines that came from farther west and went
right into the city and to the landing port. The
enormous pipelines probably carried thousands of
gallons of product in a few seconds, and that was
how the refined products were delivered for
transport off the planet.

Every hundred yards or so, there was a trailer
with a white roof, which probably held
maintenance tools and crews or some kind of
workers. As the *Defiant* went over a ridge, still

following the tri-level pipelines, a cloud of brownish smoke and smog appeared ahead of them, and they headed for it.

Huge refineries up ahead were the source for the brown cloud. Bram saw three of the large structures and wondered if there might be more, and he nodded to let Daika know to zoom over that way. As the ship moved close to the refineries, even though Bram had almost no experience with the oil industry, he could tell these were massive works. Five rail lines with the liquid carriers that held crude petroleum were lined up as far as he could see. Each liquid carrier was waiting to unload and then go back to wherever the wells were to get more crude oil. There was a cloud of refinery smog and smoke that poured out of the many smokestacks, and while he didn't ask about it, Bram wondered about environmental concerns, but that was obviously not a worrisome point for the coalition.

The ship moved slowly around the whole works, refinery by refinery.

Ogrunder spoke up to try to explain what he thought might be helpful. "Ventos is, yes—how you say—a 'cash cow,' I think the phrase is, for the Coalition. The warlord is very protective of Ventos, and all those white-roofed trailers you see are guard shacks. Guards are used for each and every single refinery and, yes, at the landing port too, but we didn't get to see them there," he said.

Bram didn't know if that was a dig at his decision to not take part in the meeting of the officials, but then he didn't really care either. This was not about diplomacy at this point; it was about seeing what cards other player held.

"I take it that the oil industry I see—or would see all across the planet—is government owned?"

Ogrunder nodded. "Yes, the whole industry was privatized when the oligarchy broke up those three years ago. Our warlord made sure that Ventos was in his control, and that was his first planet that came into the coalition."

"And government-owned-and-controlled industry is chock full of manipulations, trading restrictions, and making sure that the planet is just that—a cash cow for Tunander. We get that, and we applaud his initiative," Bram said, and he dipped his head in a tiny bow.

Sewing up a planet to join a coalition with only one member so far must have been an interesting opportunity, Bram figured, and that was something to consider when it might be time to negotiate with the warlord.

"Take us up and out to high orbit again, please, XO," Bram said, and he ignored the gentle reminders from Ogrunder about the greeting party still waiting back at the Ventos landing port.

"We need to get the tour done today, so we're off
—where to next, please?" he asked and made sure
the XO got the coordinates too.

"Jannah is the second one today, and I will need
to insist that we do go down onto the capital's
landing area. There is no real landing port or such
things here. This is a water planet—except for the
single island continent down ... down there,"
Ogrunder said as he pointed to the landmass ahead.

The XO yawed the *Defiant* to the starboard side
and then took a long slow glide toward the
landmass ahead. It looked smaller as they got
closer, and that was, at least as Bram supposed,
because in the middle of it were huge lakes, all
ringed by a set of mountains. Or at least that's what
Bram thought it looked like, and he pointed at that
area on the continent.

Ogrunder smiled. "Those are what we call—well,
what the citizens of Jannah call—the great lakes.
They hold all the fresh water on the planet—the rest
are their salty oceans covering ninety-five percent of
the planet. And it's those great lakes that are a
source of the power on Jannah," he said.

Bram nodded and realized Jannah was much like
one of the Duos planets of the RIM Confederacy.
There, the control of fresh water meant everything
—from irrigation to drinking water to life itself. He
thought he'd heard of that kind of world as a

hydraulic empire type. He had no idea if that was correct, but he shook his head once more as the XO turned to look at him.

Instead of aiming at Royce, the capital, she took the *Defiant* down to a few thousand feet and skimmed over the ocean. Going over a very sandy wide beach, which did look inviting, she flew the ship straight over the capital and right on by. It was a small city of about a hundred thousand, he thought. From what he could see easily, it was an agricultural community. Farming was the industry here on Jannah and the water to do that was controlled by the warlord.

Neat. Simple. And an easy thing to manage. Very much a planet that wanted to stay on the right side of their warlord, Bram thought and smiled.

Ogrunder smiled back at him. "We think that millions of years ago, a huge meteor hit the continent, which we can now see as the crater's edges are those mountains, and the great lakes are in the crater center. I've actually been to them, and they are the deepest, purest water bodies I've ever seen," he said.

Alver said, "I noted that back in Royce, there were many of those white-topped trailer buildings too, just like back on Ventos?" While he didn't say anything specific, it was apparent there was a reason for that question.

"Yes, those, like the ones that are on Ventos, are the barracks buildings for security guards and military police and the like," he said.

"And that's where we're headed next, to the last of the coalition worlds—to Parauda," he said, and he smiled once more as the XO powered the *Defiant* up and off the planet.

At about high-orbit level, she kicked in the Barony Drive, and the *Defiant* pointed at the Parauda system. In seconds, they were again in high orbit but off a totally different looking planet from the last one.

Green. Parauda looked very green with huge expanses of forests interspersed with lakes and rivers and, yes, the seas that existed on almost every planet. The planet had a familiar look with all the green and blue, and yes, the white banks of clouds were there too. As the *Defiant* moved downward toward the ground, Ogrunder pointed out the way for the XO to aim. In a few minutes, they were cruising over the plains area behind a big range of mountains, covered in snow.

"It's winter here on Parauda, and that means that our military training gets even tougher. Too far away to see, but on those snowfields, we have more than twenty thousand soldiers in training. Each year, we graduate about that same number, and we then lease them out—well, the warlord does that actually—but they are in demand by all of the realms here in warlord space. Our military training is without a peer anywhere—even, I assume, in the RIM Confederacy too—so that means that we are still expanding our facilities, and it's a drain on the coalition treasury for sure. Not that it won't be handled—the Tunander knows how to do that," he said, and he nodded too. Then he nodded again, as if, Bram thought, he was trying to convince himself. But that was beyond his pay grade, and he just smiled back at him.

He asked the XO to give them a tour, and over the next few minutes, the *Defiant* found two camps with hundreds of tents in each, a full school, too, buildings, and roads, and even from up here, troops could be seen marching and doing drills.

"Been there, done that," Alver said, and that got some nods in the room.

"Home, please—well, I mean, back to Crisus, and take the pad beside the *Crimson I* if possible," Bram ordered his XO.

She replied, "Wilco," and the ship tilted back as she sent it straight up and out into the blackness of space. In less than a minute, she was talking to the landing authority and then gliding the *Defiant* back to settle beside the *Crimson I*.

Bram made small talk with the warlord group as he guided them out of the *Defiant*, and he smiled a lot. He nodded when he was supposed to and then waved goodbye too, as the group led by Ogrunder waved back and moved off to get in a small bus parked there waiting for them.

Afterward, he asked Alver and the XO for their impressions of the three worlds they'd visited in a couple of hours, and he added them to his own thoughts and sent an EYES ONLY with the combined comments to the duke before dinnertime.

Tonight, Bram would have dinner at a local restaurant that came very well recommended by Ogrunder and his crew, and then it'd be an early night. *At least early to bed,* he thought.

Bram worried if he'd spend yet another night with some tossing and turning. He often thought about how Gia was and wondered what she knew about him. *I'd like to put my name on her visitor's list to be vetted by the ducal courts ... if she would even see me.* Right now, Bram was sure of only one thing, and it was not something he could ignore.

The EYES ONLY flashed on the screen, and moments later, the Duchy d'Avigdor's icon of the three planets appeared, and just as quickly, it faded as the duke's face came on screen.

"Hello all," Tanner said, and he nodded to them

from his private study in the ducal palace. Out of
camera range, but still able to partake in the
conversation, sat Helena, his wife, who was wolfing
down some lunch. At least Tanner thought it looked
like lunch, but there were too many tentacles in it
for his liking.

Captain Sander smiled back at Tanner and said,
"Hello too, Your Grace. We are all here—myself;
Daika, the *Crimson I*'s XO; Lieutenant Walton, the
ship's science officer; and Major Stal as well," he
said. They were all crammed into his ready room
and angled around the monitor screen and camera
so the duke could see them as well.

"Right," Tanner said. "Then tell me about this
warlord—Tunander—and his coalition." He wasted
no time and got right to the point.

Bram filled him in, and he began with their
original reception on Oirus and then down in the
city of Crisus. He talked at some length about his
group's feelings about the "banana republic" feel of
this warlord and his home planet. Tanner did ask
some pointed questions about the warlord himself,
which the group had some difficulty in answering.
"Mostly, we can't say much about him," Bram said,
"because we'd yet to really sit and talk with the
man, having more dealings with his aides like
Ogrunder who seemed to have attached himself to
our group."

Bram let Daika then spend a few minutes showing the duke what the various changes were since she'd been there on the *Scavenger* those five years back. Again, the duke asked some more questions, and he was surprised to hear that the latest information on Gallipedia was updated just one month back.

After Daika finished, Bram again took point, and he explained all about their trip yesterday. "The first planet we toured, Ventos Prime, had huge oil reserves and production. It is a certain winner in any realm's group of planets, and from what I could see, technology was a bit behind but still serviceable. It gets the crude to the refineries and then down to the landing ports for transport off world."

The duke nodded, made some notes on his tablet, and said, "Go on, Bram."

"Yes, Sir," Bram replied. "The second planet we toured was Jannah, and it reminded all of us of the Duos world. On Jannah, the government had full control of the only source of fresh water, which made the government a god on the planet. It was a hydraulic empire type—I looked this up in Gallipedia—and that kind of world was very much an agricultural community. Farming was the main industry here on Jannah, and the warlord controlled the water to do that."

The Duke d'Avigdor nodded, but the Duchess d'Avigdor stopped Bram to ask him a question. "And the people there, on Jannah—they allow this control?"

Bram shrugged as he replied, "There is no way of knowing, Ma'am. Our guide offered up no real information beyond what we could see from a few thousand feet above the huge lakes."

That seemed to be what she wanted, and the duke nodded to Bram to continue.

"Lastly, Your Grace, we were taken to Parauda, the real strength at least in some minds here," he said as he glanced over at Major Stal, "of the warlord's power. It's a planet with one single industry—armed forces. They turn out thousands of very well-trained soldiers annually and then lease them out to any and all of the various realms in their space. Seems like—at least from what we heard—that this is a very expensive planet that as yet does not cover its costs. At least that's the feeling we all got—right, Alver?"

Major Stal leaned forward a bit. "Your Grace— we could not really see the training or the facilities, so we've no way to actually know just how good these soldiers are. But, we were told that they graduate twenty thousand a year, and all go right out the door to various realms here in Pentyaan space—rather to Warlord space, as they now refer to their real estate. I'd definitely like the chance to visit and see their facilities and check on their training right up close—and with your permission, I'll ask for that?"

The duke nodded and said simply, "Good idea, Alver—soonest too."

Bram went on. "And that's the three worlds we saw. Each has its own issues, yet each in its own way has possibilities too. Cash cow is how our guide described Ventos Prime; an agricultural revolt in waiting was Jannah; and the Parauda planet may be something we can all look into more fully after Alver has a look-see."

The duke nodded and then seemed to be reflective for a moment. "And ... is that the whole report?"

Bram smiled and shook his head. "Your Grace, we on the RIM now take the Barony Drive for granted so much that when we told our tour guide we could go to all three of the planets—in less than a few hours—he was shocked. Amazed, maybe. We put the talks about the Barony Drive on hold—or tried. But the look on their faces when we went four lights in less than five seconds was very telling. We have something just in the drive itself that they want badly. How badly, exactly, might be for the trade group you send down here to negotiate with the warlord, but I'd say it's a major, major card to play."

He went on to explain, that he'd even had their Head Engineer come up to show the group what the Barony Drive was all about; the vid showed the various parts including the two plates, the bio-gel and it's dispenser too, the engineering console app and the satellites that sat near a sun, to provide the gravity well push. He said that the Parauda group had asked the most questions, but that all were very very much interested in acquiring the Barony Drive too. Very interested indeed.

The duke nodded and then smiled at Bram. "Well, when it comes to that 'trade group,' as you called them—that's you folks right there in the room. We have already gotten the good to go on using the Barony Drive as a trade factor, so in your talks, you can decide what to do for the mission. I know, I know," the duke said, as he nodded, "you didn't know that you'd be the trade deal makers, and in that respect, you're definitely the ones we're counting on.

"I am, however, going to send along an old friend of ours—yours too, Bram—to help. I have requested that Ambassador Harmon be added to your group, and he'll arrive later today. You—the captain—are still in charge, Bram, but the ambassador can help with all the diplomatic wheeler-dealer type items too. Admiral McQueen suggested this secondment, and I agreed wholeheartedly.

Ambassador Harmon, Bram knew well, as they'd been together on the first contact trip to Enki years back. Bram had been charged with terrorism—not the case in reality, but those had been the charges. Ambassador Harmon had been instrumental in the back room dealings to get the case decided in Bram's favor. The addition of the ambassador to this mission was a great idea, and Bram shared that with the duke.

"Okay, then we're still waiting for the upcoming meeting with this Warlord Tunander. Alver, you can slide over to this military world for a look-see, and Bram, Ambassador Harmon will be there in a couple of hours. Please, keep me in the loop, and so far, team, so good … my thanks—the partners thank you too!" he said as the screen went dark and faded to black.

Bram looked at his group. "We all okay?" he asked simply.

Everyone nodded, but Lieutenant Walton did have a question.

"If it's okay with the captain, may I accompany the major on that trip to Parauda? I would like to see more about their training facilities and what kinds of technology they're using for their military training?"

"Permission granted, Lieutenant," Bram answered as the meeting broke up, and they all went their separate ways.

On the *Crimson I* bridge, Bram sat making reports, and while it was new to him as a new captain, he hated it more than even his old captain the duke had. Navy regulations said the captain had to sign off on everything. From the latest water purity report so that no crew ever got sick drinking local water that the ship had tanked in to the daily counting of all ordnance, it all had to be signed off by Bram. Nukes and all those new cases of the .454 Casull rounds were counted daily and then sent to the captain as a report. He was supposed to read each and every line of same—every single day— and then okay the report, which would notify the sender or author or both of same, and then it was archived in the ship's logs. From ammunition to water to green beans, every single thing that could be counted was. If an item could be tested, it was. Every single crewman too—from their latest health reports to physical performance reports to professional development testing and certifications —had reports that Bram had to sign off on.

"Reports mean what they mean, but surely ,there might be a better way," he said to himself as he

looked down the long scrolling list in his INBOX
and realized he'd be in the captain's chair for hours
still.

At some point during his second hour of
reviewing reports, the bridge door slid open, and
after he turned to look, he grinned and stood to
meet the latest team member personally.
"Ambassador Harmon, so, so good to have you
here. And I can say with all honesty, your skills are
needed!" he said as he held out his hand to shake
his friend's hand.

About sixty-five years old and in his prime,
Ambassador Harmon worked for the RIM
Confederacy government on Juno, and as their
senior diplomat, he was well respected. His white
hair, cut short now, Bram saw, sat on top of a well-
tanned face, and as always, the ambassador looked
lean, trim, and fit. In his brown civilian suit, he
looked like an ambassador, Bram thought, and they
made small talk until they reached the ready room.

Ambassador Harmon took a seat with the
captain. "Captain Sander—so good to see you. And
congratulations on your captaincy too—first Issian,
I believe, to ever be a captain on the RIM," he said.

Bram could tell the congratulations were both
sincere and honest, and he smiled back. "The duke
appears to be unafraid of change when it comes to
the RIM, and I'm just thankful for the opportunity.

But tell me, Ambassador, any news back from the Confederacy?"

They spent almost an hour catching up on what was new. Bram and the *Crimson I* had only been away for a week, but he found some items interesting.

The ambassador mentioned that Enki was pulling out of their being a part of the Caliphate, and that was big news to Bram. It appeared that would happen officially at the next upcoming RIM Confederacy Council meeting. Bram's eyebrows rose even higher when Ambassador Harmon shared the news about the Praix and Issians looking into the Ghayth wreck and among other Praix spots on the planet. Bram asked for more information, and the Ambassador took a bit of time to provide all the updates, but he did say that the whole RIM was watching that carefully especially as there might be new technology as a result.

After they had covered all the news, Bram brought the ambassador up to date on the mission. He shared what he'd been charged with on behalf of the three partners—the Duchy d'Avigdor, the Barony, and the Caliphate. He related what they'd found out so far with their first foray into Warlord space and the Tunander Coalition including what they'd seen on the coalition planets. "Some things had been explained to us, but as the visits were very

short, the explanations weren't very detailed,"
Bram said.

The ambassador nodded. "So, Captain, it
appears that we—well, you and your team that is—
will be the ones making any offers to these four
planets. Either as a whole—they can all join the
RIM Confederacy—or in part if, say, only one
wants to leave this Warlord space and come over to
our Confederacy. All I need to do, it sounds like, is
to offer some of the finer points of diplomacy—if
needed.

"And after listening to you and your overall
impressions of what you refer to as a 'banana
republic,' I think we're going to make some
headway. Nothing attracts new realms to the RIM
more than advantages that they not only do not
have but cannot get on their own—the Barony
Drive as you stated is a major negotiation tool for
us," he said.

While he was talking, Bram grinned, and in his
mind, he could see the ambassador rubbing his
hands together. *The duke had been right in getting this
diplomat along for the ride, of that, I am sure.*

Ambassador Harmon questioned Bram about
what he thought of the three worlds they'd toured.
Even though there hadn't been much time to gather
in-depth detail, Bram mentioned every single item
he could recall to try to give the ambassador as

134

much information as possible.

Toward the end of their discussions, a chime sounded on the ready room monitor, and Bram leaned to his side to click the keyboard. His bridge Ansible officer, Lieutenant Brush, had called him.

"Sir, there is an incoming Ansible message from —well, I take it that this is true—the agricultural ministry on Jannah. They're up in orbit, and after they come down, they're requesting a meeting with you. They specifically asked for it to be private, Sir. What do I reply?"

A questioning look on his face, Bram turned to the ambassador. "What counsel can you provide here, Ambassador? This is unusual to a degree, but the 'private' part is what is really worrisome, I'd think," he said.

The ambassador nodded back to him and offered up his advice. "Take the meeting, but have them okay that I can sit in on same—else refuse. That kind of a binary choice, right up front, establishes that you are willing to listen—but that you too have protocols that you need to follow. That should not be an item that they will be disliking, I'd think ..."

Bram thought about that for a second and then clicked the answer button on the keyboard in front of him. "Lieutenant, tell them that the meeting is okay but that I will also have Ambassador Harmon with me—and that's my choice. Put it nicely but make sure they understand that he will be a part of the meeting. Got it?" he asked and the "Wilco" came back strongly from his Ansible officer.

Moments later, the "meeting confirmed" notice icon appeared on the monitor.

Bram grunted. "That one worked fine, Ambassador—now let's go find a conference room we can use."

They left the ready room, and on the way through, Bram let his science officer, Walton, know they were heading down to a conference room on Deck Two, and he asked him to notify the head steward to meet them there.

After receiving an affirmative reply, Bram and the ambassador exited the bridge and walked over to the lift to go down from Deck Twenty to Deck Two, and while the trip took all of two minutes, when the lift door opened up, the head steward stood in front of them. Two of Alver's marines were there to escort the guests to whichever conference room they'd be using, and he nodded to them.

The steward gestured down the curved corridor ahead and spoke up. "Sir, we're just opening up conference room four for our use—we'll set it up quickly for, say, a group of ten at the table—five per side. We'll also have extra audience chairs behind the one side in case the visitors have more than five attendees. We're bringing down—from the kitchens up on Deck Fourteen—refreshments. Drinks like juices and waters and even wine—if that might be needed. We're also adding in some small hors d'oeuvres, too, in case the visitors might be hungry," he added.

"Or us," the ambassador said. "You run a great ship, Captain!" He smiled as they rounded the curved corridor to the conference room.

The room was bright and even cheerful, Bram noted, and he made a small request of the ship's AI to put a streaming feed of the planet Jannah up on the view-screen in a loop. That had been recorded just yesterday on their coalition tour, and he thought it a nice idea to show his guests too.

Bram and Ambassador Harmon seated themselves in two chairs, side by side on one side of the table, and noted that a steward was distributing desk pads, paper pads, stylos, and pens for each of them and then for the five places on the others side of the table. Another was putting up fresh empty glasses and pitchers of water on each side. And still others were moving trays of finger foods onto a catering table against the far wall with a side area already stocked with drinks.

My crew is pretty good, Bram thought. He'd never been a captain before, and usually when he walked into a meeting, all this had already been done.

Ahead of time. Perfect in every way. But now, he realized that a ship needed more than a captain—the crew was just as important as he was. If the Jannah world guests were impressed, it was because of the stewards. "Good thing to know," he said to himself and he nodded to the ambassador.

"I have no idea why they're coming—but I can tell you that we were supposed to land and meet all of their officials yesterday, and I ditched that idea and we flew over. I don't know what's coming, but it might well be hurt feelings, perhaps?"

The ambassador shook his head. "Not at all, Captain. The word private tells me that they're interested in something much more important than berating you about not landing. Much more, but let's see, shall we?"

Bram nodded as the last stewards finished their tasks, and the room looked nicely set for their guests who appeared to be running a bit slower than he'd expected.

"AI, can you tell me if the ship from Jannah has landed here as yet?"

The AI chimed and answered, "Captain, it appears that the ship is being held up. Landing authorizations from the landing authorities are being withheld for a reason we do not know ..."

"Now that's interesting," the ambassador said, and they waited for whatever might come next.

#####

Above Amasis, in the Barony realm, where a
space station hung in low orbit, a Caliphate ship
was in the process of docking. As usual, it had
asked for docking times and had requested a direct
connection to the station rather than being moored
off. By docking directly with the station, one could
simply walk from the *CN Roc* directly onto the
station when the airlocks were opened. The *Roc* was
a destroyer at more than eleven hundred feet in
length, which meant the helmsman needed to be an
expert as he piloted the destroyer toward Docking
Wing 4R.

The Caliph watched carefully on the view-screen
on the bridge and smiled as the huge destroyer
sidled up to the assigned docking wing perfectly.
The settling that happened via the thrusters was
almost unnoticeable, and the AI chimes on the
bridge chimed three times. The sidebar on the view-
screen noted the docking was successful, and
moments later, it showed the airlocks were now
conjoined and all was fine.

"Nicely done, Helmsman," the Caliph said, and
he got up and stretched. Since the Barony Drive
had come along, space travel had been so easy and
so quick that he almost missed the old speeds of
travel where one had to take weeks to get to

anywhere. This was certainly progress, and for that, he knew he had to thank the Barony.

But he really couldn't; after all, the Baroness had simply found the Barony Drive over on Ghayth—and while she did make it available to all the RIM Confederacy realms, that too was in her own best interests.

No matter what he felt for the Baroness, it wasn't his goal to be anything but the next chairman of the RIM Confederacy—and that meant he had to build up the Caliphate by at least six more realm worlds. It would have been only five more, but the sudden Enkian decision to leave the Caliphate had hurt his long-term goals. That, and the loss of the mining of the Xithricite on Enki, meant the Enkians could trade those rights for technology and favor from any realm on the RIM.

He sighed as he left the bridge, giving the comm to his XO and shaking his head at the request to accompany him. He went out and down the curved corridor to the lift, down to Deck One, and then down another curved corridor to the landing bay. There, he did return a salute or two, but his mind was on the upcoming surprise talk, and he walked right down the airlock ramp, stepping across the threshold to the station, and was followed by two Ramat guards.

He had wondered at bringing them along, but he

did know that to be seen walking in a public space station without guards would raise eyebrows. This was the lesser of the two evils, and he smiled at that.

He walked along the wing that jutted out of the station for the fifty feet it took to get to the actual public areas, went through the Customs checkpoint without even nodding to the officer stationed there, and turned to his left. Ahead, down the corridor, were the usual kiosks with civilians who were shopping. He knew there was a huge shopping mall area counter-clockwise to where the *Roc* had docked, but he wasn't going that way. In that direction were the major shopping stores for off-world goods, restaurants, and the big Caliphate casino. As in all space stations, the Caliphate had the monopoly of running the only licensed gambling casinos, and that legacy for his realm ran back more than six hundred years. Revenues were strong still as humans especially were susceptible to the "get rich quick" casino gaming opportunities—even though the numbers were always against them.

He smiled at that. He wondered how one could pull the handle on a slot machine if one knew it paid off so seldom that it was just burning your cash. He shook his head at that, but then he realized, as always, gambling paid for the Caliphate and his livelihood too.

He walked and nodded a couple of times when civilians pointed at him or smiled and asked if he would please have a photo taken with them—and he complied each and every time. *No sense,* he thought, *of being anything but accommodating today— the time for leadership is upon me.*

He reached the administration area after a long and very happy walk, and he entered the doors and presented himself at the reception desk. A Barony Navy lieutenant behind the counter looked up at him for a second and then back down at the papers in front of her. He shrugged. *The realization that I am someone whom she might want to get up and look after ASAP should come to her soon,* he thought Just as he thought that, she pushed back away from her desk, sputtering as she got up and rushed to the counter.

"Caliph—I am so sorry—I didn't know—we had no idea that you were going to come in here," she said as she half-bowed to him. Not knowing what else to do, she grabbed some brochures that sat on the counter-top and struggled to get them in a nice neat pile.

He nodded to her. "Yes, I am sorry, but I would like to know if I might have a few minutes with one of your staff here, Captain Magnusson?" He looked down at her from his height of more than half a foot taller than six feet.

She almost quivered as she replied, "Yes, of course, Caliph—I can page him and get him here in seconds—would you like to wait in his office while I do that, Caliph?"

He nodded and she showed him around the reception counter and across the large office to a side hallway. They walked down that hallway to the last door on the left, and she opened it up and ushered him in. He told his Ramat guards to wait in the hallway, and they took up picket positions on either side of the door as he entered.

"The captain is new here, and so he's just getting settled," she said, as she gestured around the room.

The office was small and completely barren of any kind of personality. There was a bookcase with no books—nothing, in fact, on any shelf. A filing cabinet that had two drawers half-open had nothing inside. A desk with a matching credenza was bare. There was no desk pad, photos in frames, or any personal items belonging to the captain. There was an INBOX, the Caliph saw, but it was empty. There was a monitor, keypad, and a tablet sitting neatly lined up and turned off.

He smiled at the lieutenant as he sat in the only guest chair facing the desk. "Thank you, Lieutenant—if you'd be so kind as to ask the captain to join me? And I won't keep him long either," he said politely.

She nodded, said, "Wilco," and hurried out the door.

It did take almost fifteen minutes, he noted on his PDA, but eventually, the door to the office opened, and Captain Magnusson walked in. There was a look of confusion on his face, but he said nothing until he was seated at his desk. Leaning forward on his forearms, he looked at his guest and an eyebrow arched up. "Caliph—I am more than pleased to greet you and say welcome to the Amasis space station. Had we known that you were coming by, I could have arranged a more suitable welcome for a head of state," he said.

The Caliph smiled as he noticed Magnusson's eyebrow remained raised. "Captain, yes, I am sorry. But I decided only today to come to Amasis —and it's not to be greeted by officials that I came by. I came to see you, Captain—you and you alone," he said. He leaned back, crossed one boot over the other, and smiled again at him.

"Well, Caliph—you have me at a disadvantage as I've no idea why you'd want to see me—me personally, that is," Magnusson said.

He was even more interested now, the Caliph could see. "I have a story to tell, Captain, and I want you to hear it—let me finish completely, so no interruptions, if you please?" he asked, and he got a nod from the captain.

"Fine," the Caliph said. "I have been following your career in the Barony Navy now for a few years, as your abilities and skills were noted as being above normal by our intelligence agency. Then this whole Praix situation happened. You were—as you well know when you search your own consciousness—not in charge when you shot that alien. You were in the control of the Issians— and at your trial, that was proven out of the mouth of the Issian Master Adept. She did go on to say that they could have used almost anyone at that Mexican standoff—but you were chosen. The trial found you not guilty. So there should have been no reprisals or retribution toward you from the Barony Navy."

He paused and waved his arm around the sterile office. "And this is where your admiral—we believe on orders from the Baroness—puts you for further duty. Here. Alone. In exile, I'd say."

The Caliph shook his head and continued. "So far, do I have a good grasp of your own feelings on this matter? That because of the Issian interference with you—you are now branded as an officer with little future in the Barony Navy—that those admiral's stars are no longer on your horizon?" He leaned back and motioned to the captain.

The captain just stared at him for almost a full

minute, then sighed, and shook his head. "You seem to have captured my own thoughts exactly, Caliph," he said and sighed.

Doesn't know what else to say, the Caliph thought. . The office itself, and its obvious lack of décor and personal items, spoke more than any kind of denial from him might have. *Good to know he agrees with my assessment. Now, time to pitch.*

"So, I have an offer for you. You resign your Barony Navy captaincy, today, with the station commander. You will then simply walk with me back to the *Roc*—and we will return to Neria. I offer you a rear admiral position, directly under the Caliphate admiral, Abu al-Hasan. You will earn the full admiral's rank, I'd think, within a year—but more importantly, you'd become, once again, a valuable navy officer—instead of being exiled here babysitting a space station."

He had spoken slowly, and now, he slid a small black box across the empty desk and put it right in front of the captain.

Captain Magnusson looked shocked. His face was pale, and there was a teensy tic on one of his eyelids, but he rubbed that away in a second with one hand—as the other reached out for that box. He opened it and within lay a single silver star.

An admiral's star.

He stared at it for a few seconds and then

grinned as he closed the box. "If what you said you
see was not exactly what I see too—the exile here
on the Amasis station via no fault of my own means
my Barony Navy career is over—I would not
accept this star." He pulled the closed box back
toward him and snapped a salute. "Caliph—your
newest admiral accepts your offer and will, yes,
accompany you back to the Caliphate today," he
said.

The Caliph acknowledged his salute and smiled.
The job today is done.

"I expect big things from you, Admiral. Big, big
things and—as you may or may not know—in the
Caliphate Navy, we are realists. We see and we do
what works. I would expect that same type of
characteristics from you as well."

The new Admiral Magnusson smiled, still
clenching the black box in his hand.

The Caliph stood, and before he turned to leave
his new admiral, he smiled once more. "Resign. Get
your gear over to Docking Wing 4R—where the
Roc is docked. We leave when you're aboard,
Admiral. And don't think that you're going to be
living at the same pace on Neria as you were here.
Lots of information for you to take in—including
our newest mission to Pentyaan space—which I
want you involved in soonest …"

Magnusson nodded and escorted the Caliph to

his office door. "Will report on the *Roc* in less than an hour, Caliph—and I would also like to thank you for this opportunity."

"Not at all, Admiral. I know talent when I see it —and you're going to be a positive influence in the Caliphate Navy—that's for sure ..." he said as he left the office.

Magnusson went back to sit in his chair, and he opened up his tight grasp on the box in his left hand.

"A star. An admiral's star ..." he said to himself— over and over.

CHAPTER FIVE

As usual, Beedles caused the big stink on the wreck on Ghayth, and he was not apologizing for anything.

"I said it and I'll say it again. The Praix are telepaths—and the ship is now on. That means that he can simply talk to the ship's AI without us even knowing—is that point not obvious to you all?"

Beedles stood with his hands cocked on his hips at the entrance to the ship and looked at the whole xeno team. He did not look at the Praix who stood well above him nor his Issian handler either. While the Issian had heard him, he had already stated he didn't believe that a race with fifty millennia of civilization would not be able to both hear and understand the world around them as well as what was said in their hearing too. His argument to keep the Praix out of the ship was already being surpassed by his refusal to allow the xeno team with their Praix and Issian guests inside.

"As usual," Professor Reynolds said, "you're making a stink when there's nothing to smell, Ned. Stand down, lad, or just get the hell out of the way." He walked toward Beedles.

Beedles shook his head and then moved out of the way. "I don't want to have to say I told you so —but I will, you know!" he bellowed at them and grumbled as he fell in line.

Reynolds led the way followed by the Issian and then the Praix. Two marines, who were there to watch the Praix more than anything else, walked behind the Praix with the rest of the xeno team and Beedles trailing at the end. When Reynolds reached the main walkway in the wreck, he turned to the right toward the rear cargo areas, and no amount of grumbling and complaints from Beedles were acknowledged. They went directly down to walkway number nineteen on the starboard side of the ship, taking almost fifteen minutes for them all to get to the big bank of doors.

Some were closed still, but Reynolds led the way to the second set of open doors, and they all walked inside. Smaller rooms were spaced around the interior, and he went right up to the first of those rooms.

"Can we ask, please," he addressed the Issian, "what this room holds—oh, and in all cases, we'd like to know if the contents of any room are still usable? That is, unbroken?"

The Issian, an inner circle apostle named Jana Jelinek, said, "I will ask for you," and she turned to the Praix.

Moments later, she nodded, but Reynolds wasn't sure that the Praix understood this human nonverbal sign, but that was something to think about another day.

"Yes, he says that this room holds what we call ammunition—it and the room next to it are the ship's armory. And yes, both the weapons and the ammo are both viable and active. He did caution us on using any of them though as it appears that— what do you call it—the sighting of the weapons is a telepathically controlled function only."

"Figures," Beedles said from the rear.

"Enough, Ned, or I'll have the marines take you out of the ship," Reynolds said.

More muttering came from the area at the rear, but Reynolds led the group to the next room, which according to the Praix held the weapons.

"Can you ask what kind of weapons these are? Projectile? Needlers? Stun guns? Oh, and the ranges too, if you can drill down," he said as he ensured that his PDA was recording the whole tour today.

The Issian looked way up at the Praix, and this silent conversation took more time, but eventually she once again nodded to Reynolds. "There are more than a dozen kinds of weapons here, I'm told. Lasers, projectile, needlers too. They do not have stun guns, I would suspect, as that term he did not know. There are more than three hundred here in the room on displays, as we can see, as well as behind same too. Take one down, and it's immediately replaced by the ship's AI, and the shelf once again holds the same weapon. Range he had some difficulty with too—he said if a Praix can see the target, then that's how far it can shoot—or well, thoughts to that effect. I am not that sure about this, but he seemed to think that all weapons —ours included—would be like that."

The marines with them shook their heads but said nothing, and they went on to the next room. In it were the round metal plates in groups of thirty-one. Each group had a different color, and each was hanging on the wall, except for one bare spot. But before anyone could ask, Reynolds went past the room and down a side hallway. There, in plain view, sat a round metal plate with what looked like a perch on top, and below it, an amber light shone down at the floor.

"I think that the number thirty-one is also a base

of their math, and I'd like to ask—but that can wait too, I'd suppose," Professor Ellen Irving said after getting a "quit it" stare from Reynolds who shook his head. He was the one in charge, and his look said conversation about base math with the Praix could surely wait.

Beedles spoke up from his new position right beside the Issian. "Tell him that we think that this is a Praix ladder—you simply slap one of those round plates under the perch, and it pushes the perch up to a certain level. Different colors mean different heights. Do we have that right?"

Apostle Jelinek nodded, and moments later, she nodded to him a second time. "That's what the Praix just said, yes, it's anti-gravity run and never fails, is always powered too. I haven't asked him about either of those two items—I would suspect that's for another big conversation. We, here in this galaxy, have never invented anti-gravity—nor for that matter free infinite power either. Might I suggest that those two topics be left for another time?" she asked.

Reynolds looked at his team and all nodded. Beedles grumbled once more, but eventually under Reynolds stare, he too agreed.

They walked farther into the cargo holds, and as room after room came up for investigation, the Praix simply answered what he was asked. A few times, he did offer that what was there was now older technology; it had been updated in the time between the crash of the ship those twenty millennia ago and modern times. Reynolds double-checked his PDA and made sure that it was recording all of that too.

As they finished up in the big cargo bay, Professor Scholes spoke up as they were leaving the cargo bay doors. "Is it time for the bridge now?"

They'd all known that was one item requiring complete and further study. However, taking a Praix, even one under the watchful eyes of their armed marines, into a live bridge area was something that was rife with the chance for a threatening situation to occur.

"Let's call it a day. We've notes here to transcribe, and I need to send off that report to the powers that be, so let's pick it up tomorrow in the AM with the bridge tour," Reynolds said.

All nodded and they slowly went back down walkway nineteen to where it joined with number one and then exited the ship.

#####

As it had been instructed to, the AI in the conference room said, "Captain, there are three members of the agricultural ministry from Jannah on their way in to meet with you, and they should be there in less than a minute."

Typically, the AI on any ship spoke with a male voice and with no discernible accent or distinguishing characteristic at all. As he was now a captain, Bram wondered if he could have the AI's voice changed. *Maybe the AI voice could be changed to a DenKoss fish voice,* he thought, and that almost made him laugh right out loud, but he suppressed that as the door to the conference room opened.

Two Provost guards moved to either side, and in walked the XO and then the Jannah group.

He tried not to raise his eyebrows, but he did think of Tillion for a moment as these were certainly more than well-dressed diplomats. Unlike the Tillions, they didn't wear hats, but all had shoulder-length brown hair. They were all about five and a half feet tall, of average size and weight, but the clothing had him staring.

The pants and boots were bright, bright silver shades topped with jet-black short coats. I he thought. A mandarin collar was tight around each neck with an insignia on the collar fringes. Down the front of the jacket were two rows of silver buttons only inches apart but all done up tightly. Each cuff had matching silver buttons, but only three in a row so the cuffs could perhaps be undone and rolled up. On the chest was nothing, but just below it were two big slash pockets that ran right around to the sides. *Looks just plain uncomfortable ... and hot, Bram thought,* as he and the ambassador rose to meet their guests.

The XO looked after the introductions, and they exchanged handshakes as was the custom on Jannah, Bram thought, and then everyone took a seat as the XO left them and sealed the doors behind her.

The agricultural minister, Anatole Markulin, as he'd been introduced, was now seated in the middle of the three, and he leaned forward to speak first.

Before he could even take a breath, Ambassador Harmon interrupted him. "So very nice to have you here with us—even though this was a surprise, we do welcome you all and would have you note that over there," he said as he gestured toward the close wall and the catering table, "we have some light refreshments and drinks of juice or water. Plus right in front of you, there are pitchers and glasses of local Oirus water too, should that appeal more to you."

The Jannah people nodded and then all except for the minister looked over at the tables. The minister's eyes never left Bram's, and he once again leaned forward to speak after nodding to the ambassador. Bram thought it was an almost "thanks but no thanks" kind of nod, but he did give the minister the benefit of the doubt.

156

"Captain, we come to you today in the hopes that a frank and honest discussion might be possible. We were so disappointed that yesterday you chose not to stop to meet with us and just to fly over Jannah. So we immediately got in our fastest ship to come here as directly as possible. Of course, we do not have the speed that this ship does—we use the regular TachyonDrive and it did take quite a bit more time—but we do need to speak to you. You are RIM Confederacy representatives, correct?"

Bram nodded and said, "Yes, we are here in your Warlord space to begin talks with any realms that might be interested in trade discussions with the RIM Confederacy. Might that be of interest to you, as representatives of Jannah?"

That put it right in his lap, Bram thought and he waited ... and waited while the agricultural minister seemed to be weighing that query.

He must have come to some answer in his own mind as he eventually nodded and provided his own thoughts. "We seek frank discussion. We carry, with us, the full authorization of the Jannah local government to begin discussions, yes, to seek trade opportunities with the RIM. More importantly, we are also under some time constraints as well so that may have a bearing on our talks," he said.

Time constraints, Bram knew, in any kind of

negotiations usually gave one side a huge
opportunity to cut a deal that was much more in
their own favor. If this minister did not know that,
then he shouldn't be sitting at the trade deal table.
Yet here he was. That caused Bram some anxiety,
but he chose to ignore that for now.

"Might we ask up front—and I think I have this
correct—but you here today speak on behalf of
Jannah. And that is the planet itself—and not for
any part of the Tunander Coalition. Correct?"

The three Jannah representatives across the table
from him all nodded in unison.

"Then I guess I'd now like to ask what is it you
have in mind—just as a way of us getting some of
the facts on the table, so to speak?" he followed up
with.

The minister smiled just a touch. "We—Jannah
that is—are interested very much—greatly one
might say—in the technology that we only recently
learned is available only in the RIM Confederacy,
from the planet called Hope. At least that's what we
think is the name of the planet who has this
technology. Might I ask—are you at all familiar
with what is called ion-exchange membrane
desalination?"

Bram and Ambassador Harmon, who sat beside
him, shook their heads.

"Very well, in any case, what we want is that

brand new technology for Jannah. The planet of Hope is a water planet much like our own with more than eighty percent coverage of oceans. And the people of Hope have invented, we understand, a way to use free solar power to force the salt ocean waters through an ionic membrane—removing all salt and chlorine atoms from the resulting pure water. This pure water can, of course, be drinking water—but more importantly for Jannah, it can be irrigation water. Water that up until now, we pay far too much for which affects our whole planetary economy." He sat back then and waited.

Bram thought about what he'd just heard and mulled it around. *Sounds like these Jannah folks think the coalition charges far too much money for their use of irrigation waters for the agricultural-based economy. That means Jannah is looking for a change—and the simple import of the Hope distillation technology would do more than give them much cheaper water—it would probably mean they'd be leaving the Coalition as that change would not be allowed by Tunander.*

Before Bram could address that, Ambassador Harmon spoke up.

"We understand then what it is you're after—and while neither of us, I believe, has information on that Hope technology, might we ask then why there might be some kind of time constraint with this trade item?"

Bingo, Bram thought. *Yes, let's get all their cards on the table.*

The minister nodded and put it simply to them. "We are in the middle of harvests on Jannah. Next season will be our winter, so the lands are fallow, and then the next season, it's planting time and then growing season—and that takes water. Millions and millions of gallons of water, I would add."

Ah, that explains the time constraints, Bram thought. "So, Minister, what you're interested in," he said, trying to find a way to get the man to lay all his cards down, "is the Hope solar distillation technology. But what can you offer in its place that might be of equal value?"

They sat for a moment, and then one of the other Jannah representatives nudged the minister and said in a very audible whisper, "Do it, Anatole," and the minister nodded in response.

"If that technology holds out the promise we need, we would then not need the—the 'protectorship' that the coalition offers us now. We would become a realm looking to become a full RIM Confederacy member or even a realm of a current one.

"I am sorry—I know that this is so sudden ... but you must understand the huge issues that play out on Jannah every season, and we'd be more than prepared to sit down with whomever the RIM

Confederacy might want to discuss this in detail. Might I also add that this is frank discussion—but we ask that it remain among us here in the room only. Confidential, that is?"

That got a quick nod and agreement from both the ambassador and Bram.

The Jannah cards were out on the table all right. They wanted to trade and at the highest level. Bram wondered what to say next, but he lost the opportunity to speak next when the minister suddenly rose.

"The Tunander knows we were here. He knows that we talked. So our story is that we came here in person to meet with the RIM Confederacy diplomats and to tell them what a wonderful planet that Jannah is—and to make a date for a real live tour of the planet in the next few weeks. That is our story, and if I could ask, if you back this up, then that should alleviate any thinking else-wise on the Tunander's behalf."

Bram thought that this too was smart, and he agreed to same in a heartbeat. They made small talk about Jannah, specifically how beautiful it was with the planet's two full moons shining down on those great lakes and the snow-covered mountains around them in the winter.

Moments later, their guests had left, and Bram and the ambassador were standing alone in the open bay of the landing deck. They turned to face each other.

"Guess I need to do some investigation on the Hope technology," Bram said.

That got a nod from the ambassador. "And I'll see if I can find out if there is a Tunander Coalition Constitution or something similar. If Jannah wants out, then we'd like that to be as simple as possible without any threat of violence."

That got a nod from Bram, and they spun to go back across the landing deck to take the lift up to the bridge.

#####

She seldom did this, but this time was different. She lay on the warm beach sand with a coconut drink at her side. *Probably in the eighties today,* she thought, *but that's just fine. Can request a cold drink ... anything, really ... whenever I want.*

Owning a resort meant she was able to just Ansible in a request for anything from a cold drink to the biggest and best accommodations, regardless of who might be staying in same. Hustled off, and stuffed full of credits, the honeymoon couple who had left not two hours ago would have a great story to tell their kids in the years to come. She had the big suite, and the resort staff did nothing but watch her for any sign she might be missing something or want something.

The fact that she was the Baroness, and that the planet belonged to her too, was another thing. She smiled and one finger curled up against her thigh as the long fingernail scratched an itch. Her bikini was about the smallest she'd ever seen, and there was no one here to appreciate it. *Well, no one other than staff,* she thought, *and they didn't count.*

She scratched once again on that spot, but this time with all the perfectly manicured fingernails on her right hand. The itch went away.

She grinned to herself as she thought she could have called a beach boy to help her with that. "A beach boy," she said to herself, and she smiled once more. She sighed as the light breezes wafted over her, fluttering the edge of her towel against her leg.

A few minutes ago, she had looked off toward the horizon. Bottle was a world of blue. Blue pools. Blue bar counters. Blue ocean. Blue sky, and the horizon was a lifetime away but blue.

She wondered if noticing that meant she too might be blue as well. *Probably not. I have every single thing I ever wanted. I handled my future as it came and knew when to make a move and when not to—but that hadn't happened much. Opportunities came and I grabbed them.*

She thought—or she admitted—that she felt that she was quite talented at choosing the people to

surround herself with. While some, like the late
baron, couldn't see her mind because of the body in
front of him, which had been the key for her to get
out of the pleasure trade. The day after he had
visited the pleasure gardens she had worked in,
he'd asked her to marry him, and she had done so.
In fact, he had begged her and told her about what
Royal life could be for her and that as his wife, she
would be the most important thing in his life—more
than any of his planets—and more, he had said,
than his own daughter, the Lady St. August.

His daughter was now the Duchess d'Avigdor as
well as the heir to the Barony too.

One day, she knew, the Barony and the Duchy
d'Avigdor would be one—merged via the Royal
line.

She smiled again. *Beach boy. I like that term. Not
that I have any needs for a male in her life. It is so much
more fun parading in front of them and watching their
reaction. Males of any species are so easy to tease ... and
then to bend to my will.*

She sighed one more time as she thought about
the daily EYES ONLY report she'd taken during
her breakfast this morning.

Over an ample serving of vanilla yogurt with
granola and some of those delightful Garnuthian
pecans, she'd started up her tablet and glanced at
the news from Neres City. It appeared not much

The RIM Confederacy: Inwards Bound

was new. There was an issue over on Ishtar with some rare earth import duties, and she'd delegate that one. Prime Minister Lazaro had requested a meeting over upcoming union issues that he had said might cause his economy a reset, and she'd agree to that but would need her labor advisers there as well—and she gave that one to her aides to set up.

There was a note about a conference she might want to consider over on Conclusion, and again, the aides would handle that. She nodded over the rest and noted there was no news from Ghayth and the Praix-slash-Issian tour as yet. But down at the bottom of the report, she did see a note from Admiral Vennamo. She drilled down on that one, as navy news was always well worth the read.

Her admiral shared that Captain Magnusson had resigned his captaincy in the Barony Navy. She thought about that for a moment before she finished the report.

Magnusson had impressed her when she had first learned about the man. He seemed to be eager for promotion as his ambition was a major force in his life. She had given him some direct missions, and he'd been well worth the interest. But then the Praix attack had gone so wrong. She knew that as the captain of the *Defiant*, he'd surely been one of the major forces that had gotten her marines to the

exact spot to confront the Praix. But the
unexplained attack by him on the Praix was
unexplained until his court martial, and that was
the real eye-opener, she knew.

The Issians had controlled him, like a robot, she
thought, to do their bidding, which was a total
surprise. No one had seen that as even a remote
possibility, but there it was for all to see. Issians had
the power—however seldom used—to control them
all. *That is something I'll have to consider more—not
today on the beach but back at home with wine.*

She went back to the report and had been
shocked to see that Magnusson had not only left her
employ in the Barony Navy, but he had accepted
an admiralty position with the Caliphate Navy.

"Argh," she had yelled, and then she had thrown
her spoon out onto the sand in front of the breakfast
patio at her resort. She hadn't cursed, which she did
pride herself on, as it was a habit she'd broken.

Magnusson was now an admiral. Instead of
accepting the repositioning that her own admiral
had fought her for—Vennamo had thought it made
no sense to take Magnusson off the admiral track
due to his unknowing culpability in the Praix
matter—she had parked him on Amasis on their
space station. Vennamo had not liked that and
made it an item she'd brought up in her weekly
talks with her.

A career parking, for sure, but still, why had the Caliph made such an offer? And why had Magnusson chosen a new career with the Caliphate Navy?

She had left her tablet on the table as she strode back to her suite and changed to go lie on the beach. Now, hours later, she still had no idea as to why this had happened and who had arranged for it either.

The Caliph? But why?

Magnusson? But why?

She tilted her head toward the surf and placed the straw coming out of the coconut between her lips. She drew a large ice-cold mouthful of the rum and coconut juice up through the straw. "Tastes great," she said to herself.

Her questions about Magnusson still bothered her. She rolled halfway to her right and propped herself up with an elbow in the sand.

Still blue out there ... still blue ...

#####

Bram had spent the day reviewing reports and working on creating the report on the Jannah agricultural meeting of yesterday. It had taken the remainder of the day yesterday for Ambassador Harmon to follow through on his thoughts of trying to find a Tunander Coalition Constitution. And there wasn't one. Like most, or perhaps all dictatorships, if that was what one might call the coalition, the constitution existed only in the dictator's head.

Bram now sat in his quarters with Ambassador Harmon to learn if the additional time had paid off. The ambassador had found some help in that, like all dictatorships, the dictator wanted to provide at least the appearance of having an arm's length distance between him and his judicial system. So Harmon had asked to see past case law and had been provided with archives of past court documents. The fact that they were poorly organized and hard to search through was the bad thing that came along with all those petabytes of data. Still, the ambassador had attempted to search, and after a long night, followed by asking for more time this morning, he had reached an answer.

"In the coalition, Bram, there is nothing preventing any member from leaving—except the power of the dictator himself. That would mean that unless there was a benefit—a huge benefit to Tunander—he'd never let Jannah go. At least that's how I see it, and the case law proves that only no one else has ever left the Tunander Coalition. Ever, was the active word there, Bram," he said as he shrugged at the same time.

"He needs to be rewarded, then. That's not surprising, based on the little that we know. But more than that, we should perhaps try to look into the coalition military strength on Jannah. Who is there and in what numbers? Plus, I just realized, we also need to do an audit on the coalition ships and their crews too, and I'll look at someone to handle that for us," Bram said.

Ambassador Harmon nodded. "I'd suggest Major Stal look at that information and give us a military opinion."

Before Bram could reply, AI chimed and announced the steward would arrive shortly with Bram's meal.

"That'll be my cue to leave," the ambassador said and stood.

Bram leaned back in his chair and crossed his arms. "I'll update you soon as there is anything new."

Shortly after the ambassador left, the steward brought in Bram's meal. Bram was ready to set up the EYES ONLY Ansible with the mission partners, but before he did that, he tried to finish his meal. Using his fork, he pushed the macaroni and cheese around on his plate. He squeezed some more ketchup onto his plate, added a swirl to a full forkful of macaroni and cheese, and tucked it into his mouth. This was one of his favorite meals. He enjoyed macaroni and cheese, and with ketchup, it was a real meal.

He tried to remember when he'd first eaten this dish and came up empty. It had always been a part of his childhood on Eons, and he remembered his nanny—a Mournful mother—had a child too that loved same. While his parents were both away at work, he remembered, the nanny would make lunch, and then while Bram ate, she fed her son who was about the same age as he was. *The boy's name was ... was ... I can't remember—wait, it was Eric.* Eric was a Mournful, and that meant that he was unable to do much for himself. He had blond hair, so blond it was almost white, Bram remembered. He remembered Eric had sat and fixated on something in front of him or near to him, and Eric had done nothing but stare at that object. He couldn't, Bram remembered now, wipe his nose or do much for himself but blink. Nanny had come in to the family room every ten minutes to look at him and make sure he was okay, but she had also paid attention to Bram too.

He hadn't thought of Eric now in more than twenty years, and he wondered whatever happened to the Mournful. Even now, thinking about the Issian word for this kind of disorder bothered him —not politically correct was how he'd put it. In fact, he now wondered more about this whole group of challenged Issians, and he decided to put it in his personal log and make it a point to discuss same with the Master Adept the next time they met.

As he chewed the macaroni and cheese, he shook his head one more time and tried to focus once again on the Tunander Coalition.

No constitution. No way on paper then for a member to leave. The only way that might work, would be to buy their way out, if the price was right for Tunander.

Bram knew it wasn't as good as it could be, but at least the decision of what to do would be made by the duke and his partners.

He used the edge of his fork to scoop up the last part of his meal, including the rest of the ketchup too. He grinned at himself as he sat looking at the view-screen on the exterior bulkhead wall. He had it set to show the exterior of the landing port, and he'd noticed there was little traffic in and out of Oirus. Too little, he thought, to indicate a viable lively economy. That was another story, but he was a navy captain and not some kind of an academic, so he put that thought away. Then he pulled it right back up front in his consciousness. Maybe he'd get the helmsman to ask landing authority for some kind of logs on the ins and outs of ships. That way, he'd at least have some stats to give to the duke too.

He slid the plate back onto the tray and said, "AI, find me my steward."

After a moment, there was a double knock on his door.

"Enter," he said, and his steward came in with a hot cup of coffee—Blue mountain he'd asked for this time—and he placed it on the desk in front of him and swept away the tray and dirty dishes.

Bram sat for a moment sipping the too-hot coffee and then sighed. He clicked the on button on his console, and the monitor came on. In moments, the Ansible officer on the *Crimson I*'s bridge appeared on the screen.

"Sir, we have confirmations for the EYES ONLY from all three of the receiving parties. Whenever you want, we can connect, Sir," he said.

He nodded at Lieutenant Brush and said, "You're good to go, Lieutenant."

Moments later, the monitor faded to black, and then there appeared four panes on the screen, and as the connections were made, the faces of the Duke d'Avigdor, the Baroness of Neres, and the Caliph of Neria appeared.

They made small talk after their hellos, and in less than a minute, the duke said, "An update, please, Captain, on what you have learned so far, if you please?"

Bram went through the notes in front of him. He remembered to thank the partners for sending him the ambassador since his help already had been fruitful. First, he went through the initial meeting with the Tunander and shared his opinion that he

172

was in fact a dictator.

Next, he related the details of his visit to the other three Tunander Coalition planets and shared his thoughts on each. He also noted their economic situations and what he—well, he and the ambassador too—thought of their future.

Bram moved on to the meeting with the delegates from Jannah. He explained that the Jannah agricultural minister had visited and had offered—well, almost offered—that they'd leave the Tunander Coalition for access to the Hope solar distillation technology. Bram shared that the Jannah representatives had expressed they had no preference whether they joined the RIM Confederacy as their own realm or joined an already established member's realms.

Finally, Bram expressed that—in his and Ambassador Harmon's opinion—one way to get Jannah to leave the coalition was to simply buy their way out and prevent any kind of violence. Bram stated that buying them out could be easy as the Barony Drive had the whole Tunander Coalition drooling for access to same. It was a bargaining chip that could be played to great advantage for the RIM Confederacy—at least in his opinion.

He stopped then and the partners had no further questions. He thanked them for their time and then signed off.

He would have loved to be a part of the conversation between the partners. But that was not to be. He'd been told earlier that the duke would send back instructions after the three of them made a mission decision based on the information Bram reported to them.

In the top right-hand corner of his monitor screen, an incoming message icon was flashing, and he clicked it and saw there was an incoming off-world request for a meeting from Parauda.

He looked out once more on the landing field. There was room for more than fifty ships, but there were exactly three—the *Crimson I,* the *Defiant,* and one ship of the line from the Tunander Coalition.

He thought it strange once again, but then all here in Warlord space had been strange. Still, he acknowledged the message and accepted the meeting time and date for the day after tomorrow in the morning.

And he sat back. *More to do, of course, like reports to sign off on and thinking on what the Parauda meeting might mean and how to prepare for it ...* he thought and sighed.

Captaincy was a great thing that had happened to him, but it seemed so much more time intensive than simply being an Adept Officer.He clicked the reports folder and sighed as he saw there were twenty-three of same waiting for his attention.

CHAPTER SIX

The ship was white—which was not that strange —but the whole ship was white. There wasn't a single different color anywhere else. Even the frigate's engine cones were white, and that was something only an engineer could arrange. Bram sighed. *Of course, it was white—weren't the Parauda colors white on white?* Bram recalled all those trailers over Ventos, Jannah, and Parauda were white too. He watched as the ship came down on its InertialDrive and landed about ten spaces over from the *Crimson I.*

He smiled as he noted that because the ship was from within the coalition, there was no greeting party of Customs and Health, nor was there any kind of official greeting party. He wondered about that for a moment and then shrugged.

Just a visit from a cousin was how he looked at it — most likely just like the Oirus landing authority did.

Works for me, he thought, and he watched on the bridge view-screen as it took about five minutes for the ship to drop her landing ramp. Four men dressed completely in white—at least as far as he could see— walked down the ramp in a marching step. They wheeled at the bottom of their ramp and then aimed over at his ship. He watched for a moment and then left the comm with his science officer.

"Major and XO, you're with me, please," Bram said, and the three of them left the bridge to go down to Deck Two and the same conference room used for the meeting with the Jannah representatives..

"Sir," Alver said, "maybe we should just have the stewards set this room on constant meeting status— seems like a way to stay ahead of whomever might want to meet next."

That got a chuckle from all three of them. Bram thanked his steward team for the quick setup and saw that it was very similar to the previous meeting. Refreshments and hors d'oeuvres had been set out, and the other side of the table held only four chairs this time.

Moments later, they were seated at that same

table with Alver to Bram's left and the XO to his
right. The door slid open and the ship's Provost
guards entered with their guests. They exchanged
introductions and then the visitors sat.

Their visitors wore white uniforms with almost
no decoration of badges, ribbons, sashes, or
shoulder epaulets. Even their sleeves had no stripes
and the buttons were plain, Bram saw. The only
way to tell who was of what rank was the single
badge on each side of their collar. It was nice to see,
Bram noticed, that the major who sat opposite him
and was the senior officer wore a gold oak leaf.

He smiled at the major and asked, "Do you care
for any refreshment?"

"Not at this time. We, instead, wish to get to our
reason for this meeting, if that would be
appropriate with you?" the major asked.

He looked to be in his mid-thirties. *So just a few
years older than me,* Bram thought. The major was of
average size, weight, and height too. He had short
hair, blue eyes, and a small scar on one very tanned
cheek.

"Certainly, we can get right to business, Major.
But we'd like to say that we did enjoy our short
flyover of your planet a few days ago. We didn't
really see much, but it is a beautiful planet, we all
thought," he said. *That was platonic enough,* he
thought.

The major nodded but barely, Bram noticed, and then he spoke in what Bram considered to be a matter-of-fact voice. "Captain Sander. We are the representatives of the Parauda Military Government. We are here on their behalf. We have been charged with the duty to bring to your attention that Parauda wishes to make an official statement to you. A statement that you will need to understand will serve as notice of action. If you—or any of your RIM Confederacy representatives— make any attempt to disrupt the Tunander Coalition in any way, then we will take you under arrest and have you or the guilty parties charged with treason. The crime of treason here in the Tunander Coalition is a capital offense and punishment will be carried out immediately upon the verdict being given, by the Tunander himself. Do you understand this official notice?"

He just stared at Bram and said nothing else. The others sat looking at him as well. No one said anything.

Bram tapped a finger on the table, as he sent out a mental tendril to search the major's mind. Unsurprisingly, what he found was as he'd thought. The major was just a messenger. All he knew was that the Parauda Military Government had given him the mission to convey the official notice. But that was not the real power there, Bram knew—this

179

came from the Tunander himself.

He would have loved to say many things, but being a captain had changed that.

"Then yes, Major, I have heard you, and I understand your notice. I do not agree with it, but that is for another day. And a small reminder, Sir, that the realms that are a part of the RIM Confederacy are generally not the kind of folks who take threats as a matter of course. We, instead, act as we always have, and what you imply might lead to an altercation. And we win all altercations—just so you know, Major," he said, and he leaned toward the Parauda soldiers and slammed his hand down on the table.

The noise made the other side of the table flinch just a bit.

Bingo, Bram thought. *They know that already. That's a good sign.*

Bram nodded and said, "This meeting is over— and just a small tip, Major. If you ever come back here looking to arrest anyone, I'd bring a lot more men than the four of you." He spat those words out, stood, and stared at them.

Everyone sitting on the other side of the table rose, turned on their heels, and walked out with their Provost guard escorts.

Bram sat back down and looked first to his XO. "Daika—any comments?"

She shrugged. "Seems that they were just here to deliver a message—but I think it comes from the coalition dictator, not their government. Shouldn't be a problem though, our own forces are so well trained and all ..." she said.

Major Stal nodded to that and added his own take on the very short meeting. "From where I sit, they, yes, were just here to intimidate us. To tell us that the Jannah meeting cannot be acted on. To tell us that they're watching. And that there may be a—what, an altercation I think you called it, Bram? And I can say my marines will make short work of them for sure," he finished off.

Bram nodded. He agreed with both of them and then thanked them for their help, and the meeting broke up. Bram took the stairs down to Deck One and then walked over to look out of the wide-open portal on the *Crimson I*'s landing deck.

Across the pads, the white Parauda ship was powering up; going home, he suspected. In moments, she climbed up on her InertialDrive and was on her way.

The duke nodded, asked an off-camera steward for a refill, and then held up his hands. "Wait ... wait. Let's not argue. Here's where we are—at least right now," he said.

The Caliph shook his head, and the Baroness nodded in agreement. The Caliph had been more than adamant that they needed to make a real solid move on their first acquisition in Warlord space. "We can't just let the Jannah world join as a full member. That—"

"Enough," Tanner said, and he tried to recount what they had agreed too—as little as it was.

Tanner was in his private study on this EYES ONLY conference call. From what he could see around the Caliph, he was in his tent palace, but Tanner didn't recognize the room. And the Baroness was on a patio, as behind her lay the well-kept Barony Palace gardens and pools, and the usual glass of wine sat beside her elbow.

"We agreed that we want Jannah to come over to the RIM Confederacy, right?" Tanner questioned.

The Caliph and Baroness agreed and nodded.

"We also agreed that if they are to leave, then that action will most likely cause the coalition to fight to keep them, right?"

Again, the two heads nodded.

"And, we also think that the only way to avoid that is to buy the planet from the coalition, so to speak—correct?"

The Baroness nodded, and the Caliph did as well.

"And the sticking point is that some of us—well,

the Caliph only—feels that we should not make the
offer to Jannah to join the RIM Confederacy on
their own—"

"Which," the Baroness interrupted, "will force
them to become a realm of a RIM Confederacy
member. Which while sounding good, is not the
whole truth," she said.

Tanner was a bit surprised by that, as he
suspected the Baroness wanted Jannah for the
Barony, but he had to take what she said at face
value.

The Caliph nodded. "We think that the way for
this first acquisition to go is—we, one of us, buys
them out from the coalition. Period."

Tanner smiled. A way ahead had just come to
him.

"Then here's what I think. We as a partnership
do not pick a way to go ahead. Instead, I propose
this idea. That if you, Caliph, or you, Baroness,
want to own the Jannah world, then you have to
make a bid for it. You set the price that you think
you need to pay—and you send to Oirus your own
delegates with your offer. Will that work for you
both? Oh, and just to help, we—the Duchy—are
going to pass on this opportunity. So that leaves
you two alone in the running. Are we all good with
that proposal?"

The Baroness sipped her wine and then looked at

the camera after studying her gardens. "I agree. The partnership is good to find these opportunities —but yes, at the basis of all this is my want to grow the Barony. So yes, I agree," she said.

The Caliph spoke last. "Agreed. We will send our team first thing tomorrow—but a reminder for our mission already on Oirus. They are not to interfere with our Caliphate diplomats. Not at all. Agreed?"

And both Tanner and the Baroness nodded.

The conference call ended. *That had gone … well, it had gone okay,* Tanner thought.

The opportunity was now before the Barony and the Caliphate. They'd each work out what they thought was the right offer and then make it. It was up to the dictator to decide.

What was unusual, Tanner thought, was that neither had come up with an alternate idea. If the partnership had chosen to invade and take over the whole coalition, they would have had four planets to divvy up. Tanner knew it might have taken some real work by their marines, but it was just another way to acquire worlds.

Tanner thought about that for a moment.

He knew that he wanted to expand the Duchy d'Avigdor—but only if the realm wanted to join them. *No force, no check, no threats make any sense to me.* That, he thought, was perfectly in line with what the late duke had believed and had done.

184

He sat there and thought about what that might entail from the discussion this evening, and his thoughts went all over.

Thoughts of Gia filled his mind, and in seconds, after making some clicks on his keyboard, he was looking down at her six rooms here in the palace.

She was in her living room, as she'd called it. She was sitting on a large pile of pillows in front of one of the couches with a tablet just to her left side. She was watching something on the big screen that sat above the fireplace right in front of her. She was often in this room, which he knew as he looked down on her from the apartment's AI almost every day.

He wanted to just walk right in and talk with her, but Doctor Etter had advised against that. Instead, he had said that Tanner must wait until she voiced that she wanted to see him. While he believed the doctor was most likely giving him solid advice, he still wanted to talk to her and voice his concerns about her health—well, her mental state, he meant.

She was twirling one strand of her blonde hair in her fingers, and her head was tilted to one side. Her attention was only on the screen, and he watched her watch her movie for more than a few minutes. Then he leaned forward and clicked the console off button.

In his study, he sat and tried to decide what to do

with Gia and wondered what she might want.

Sleep tonight was going to be tough, he thought, but he'd try, and he wondered if Gia slept well.

#####

Admiral McQueen sat, as always, in the first tier of seats behind Chairman Gramsci in the Council chamber. He realized earlier that he'd taken this seat at least once a month for the past twelve years since he'd won the job at the top of the RIM Confederacy Navy.

Twelve years here on the RIM, and life here is still a liquid environment. Things did change, but then they changed again. And again. And today, again, he thought and shrugged mentally. *That was how it was, is, and will be. Nothing for an admiral to do but to follow along and nod. And if necessary, say what he needed to say.*

Today, as he looked at his Agenda, there were no real realm-shaking items. He saw a request for a few changes to the trade rules over on Leudie and something new on the Praix issue from the Baroness. He didn't read much else that should cause a big to-do.

Speaking of to-do's, he thought, as he watched the inevitable mopping up of spilled seawater around the DenKoss members at the table. Each meeting, they were moved from their normal containers that they left their ships in, which were moved from the landing port here on Juno to Navy Hall and then up the elevator to the Council chamber. Once in the Council chamber, they were taken out of of those containers to sit—*Maybe lie might be a better verb*, McQueen thought—in their chamber seats, but they were hooked up with their own seawater respirators so that they could be in the air-breathing environment and survive. After the seating of the DenKoss members came the usual mop up of the spilled seawater, which was happening now.

We have many members from many species, McQueen thought, *and while the DenKoss fish members may be the oddest of the group, there are others.* He looked over at the Ttseens, who looked so much like the human boxer dogs he'd seen photos of that he often wondered what might happen if he threw a stick and yelled fetch! There were other strange ones too like the Djarreer who needed a perch to sit on as they were birds—or had been birds at one time.

A gavel smacked the table in front of him and broke into his thoughts listing the odd species in the room.

"Welcome all," Chairman Gramsci said, "and let's get started, shall we?"

He put the gavel down, picked up a tablet with another hand, and began to make notes while two other hands sorted through the stack of folders in front of him. "With six arms, the Alex'n citizen could really run a meeting," McQueen said to himself, and he settled in for the meeting.

"Clerk, please, any regrets for today's scheduled meeting?" the chairman asked.

She rose from her seat in the middle of the big horseshoe-shaped table and nodded to him. "Yes, Chairman, we have received notice that the member from Farth will be unable to attend—holidays there seem to have made their presence a necessity. Also, but with no reasons behind same, the Faraway member sends his regrets as does the member from Duos. The Duos Valor realm, that is, FYI," she said.

Everyone knew that the Duos realm had two major planets—Valor and Hedges—that had been at war now for almost a hundred years. Still, he was grateful that while the war had been going on for so long, the reasons it had started were now lost or forgotten, and they fought only with ground troops. *Boots on the ground rather than ships in space*, he thought.

He sighed. Why that made the war any more acceptable was an issue that he'd not been asked to face. Winning a war meant doing whatever needed to be done. Period. But these two worlds were not interested in winning, he suspected.

While he was pondering that, the meeting went on, and he was surprised when the Baroness of Neres stood up to speak. Rising in her place beside the chairman, she was aglow with some kind of soft amber color that seemed to come right out of her clothing. Her shirt and light jacket were a deep amber color, and the shine that seemed to glow right off those items was a lighter color. He smiled to himself as he thought, *that woman has the most fashion-forward style I've ever seen. If fashion-forward is even the right term. I have no idea.* The last thing he thought about was a term for how the Baroness would look, but then again, information was power, he well knew. He shook his head mentally as she spoke.

"I thank the chairman for the chance to speak earlier than the Agenda placement. I would like to update you all on the latest news from Ghayth and the Praix issue. As the report sent to you all," she said as she looked behind her and got a nod from an aide, "shows, we have made some small headway with the tour of the wreck on Ghayth. The report spells out the complete listing of the items, and you can read that at your own leisure. What I wanted to say is that we think—we do not know, but we think—that there is still something more that the Praix are not telling us.

"We already know and have shared their own

fears about this new invader over in SagD who simply arrives and then turns off stars. We already know that the Praix feared for their own survival and sent out more than a thousand ships with the intent to both run away and still conquer new galaxies. If you think about that—with their superiority in technology—that they're running away from a more superior threat is what is stunning," she said.

An interruption came from the Doge of Conclusion. "But, Baroness, as we all know—fear drives one more than any other emotion. Could it not then be assumed that their intent to also 'conquer' was a lower or secondary or tertiary goal? If one at all?" He looked like he was more than ready to argue that point, McQueen thought and to some degree, he agreed with the alien.

She nodded and then held out her hands palms up. "We don't know at all, Doge—but that is unimportant. What we do know is that they did arrive here, looking to once again get the Issians on their side. But what we don't know is why they so easily seemed to capitulate when the incident on their ship occurred. We think, and the Issians also concur," she said as she waved over to the left side of the table at the Master Adept who acknowledged that fact, "that there is something else going on with the Praix. We do not have all the facts as yet—but we continue to try to delve into this. And my reason for this aside to the report is that we felt the whole Confederacy Council should know. And so we dig deeper," she said.

The Council sat and digested that. Some were reading the report, and some were just looking at her. With no further questions, she sat, and the chairman struck his gavel once and then went on.

While the Council business moved on, McQueen spent some time trying to figure out what the Praix could be hiding. But he had no idea of what that might be. As well, he knew, as they all did, that the only ones who might know were the Issians as they were the conduit through which the Praix communicated with the Council. As he looked over at the Master Adept, she looked back at him and smiled. He nodded and then looked down once more at his own Agenda sheet. He reminded himself that sitting in a room with someone who could read minds was always going to be a challenge if one wanted to keep secrets. Out of the corner of one eye, he could see the Master Adept who continued to smile at him, and that made him sigh.

"Fine, Clerk, mark that as accepted, and please update our trade regulations to allow this exemption, please," the chairman said. Next item … number nine, I believe?" he said.

The clerk rose once again and introduced the speaker. "The Enkian ambassador, Eecesoe Qig."

Rising from the first tier of seats behind the table, a feathered alien stepped forward. Just over five feet tall, the alien had a beak instead of lips. On his feet sat big talons capped with tiny feathers. He wore a short brown jacket with the same red and blue coloration as the logo of the Enkian's muse. But it was the top of his head with its feathered crest of mixed red and blue feathers that signified that this Enkian belonged to the group known as the Fine Arts Muse that was really impressive.

"I speak today on behalf of the planet Enki. While we could spend hours on the background of this decision, the point of me rising today is to announce that we are hereby taking our Confederacy constitutionally valid choice to leave the Caliphate—effective today," he said and returned to his seat.

There was a short moment where there were some gasps and then quiet. Complete silence ensued, and McQueen knew the members in the chamber were weighing that announcement. As he looked around, he imagined he could see some light bulbs going off above heads.

The Baroness jumped to her feet. "Might I, Chairman, ask the ambassador a question?"

He nodded and she went on.

"Then as the constitution says, if this is the choice of a member of a realm to leave same—does that mean that Enki will now entertain proposals or offers to join other realms?" she asked.

Sweetly is how I'd name the tone of her voice, McQueen thought. *Wonder what she's thinking?*

Ambassador Qig rose once again and stepped down off the tier to speak to that point. "Yes, we will entertain offers from other realms, but you must all know that we are also considering the standalone possibility as well. Perhaps, it will be decided that Enki will join the Confederacy as a full member. Those talks are going on in our latest conclave—but I have been instructed to let you know that offers will be accepted with no obligation to accept any of them. That is all that I have been empowered to say," he said. He again returned to his seat.

The ledger sheet was easy to figure. Can almost hear the wheels turning in their heads as they consider this opportunity, McQueen thought.

McQueen mulled over the positives and negatives to this status change for Enki. On the plus side sat the Xithricite, the ore that could make one's ships invulnerable in space. And on the minus side was nothing he could think of other than the normal investment made in a new member to their realm— the usual items of infrastructure, ships, and trade.

He looked down and slid a hand across his chin to hide the grin he couldn't stop from appearing on his face. Still, he reasoned, the Caliph had not yet spoken on this, and he looked up and across the table at the alien.

The Caliph sat still, looking down at his tablet as though reading something. He made no public display of any kind of emotion.

Funny. Wonder why he is staying silent, he thought. *There must be a reason ... an explanation or excuse for that, and I'm sure others in the room have reached the same conclusion ...*

And as he thought that, he looked over at the Master Adept, who was looking at the Caliph with a stare ... and nothing more ...

#####

It had taken almost four days to reconvene the tour of the wreck on Ghayth as the Baroness had asked for it to be halted until further notice. Professor Reynolds had no idea why when she had asked, but in the EYES ONLY message just this morning, the Baroness had told him the why. She had wanted to report the truth and the whole truth to the RIM Confederacy Council at the meeting just yesterday. And that meant she wanted to leave out the bridge area, which was now on the schedule for today.

This morning, in fact, he had arranged for it to be done, and he hoped it was going to go well.

As the Baroness had implied, there was more that might be important on the bridge than anywhere else on the ship. So she wanted that to be hidden from the Council at least until she could digest whatever came along.

He sighed. This politicking was more than he was ever going to understand, but more than that, he believed it was just plain stupid. *What we're doing here is what a xeno team would give their eyeteeth for — the drilling down by the actual aliens who'd built the wreck.* It made sense that the technology within could be explained by its creators. Reynolds believed that should and would validate the work done by the xeno team the past year.

He looked over at his PDA on his wrist and saw the team would be assembling by the entrance to the wreck now. He stood from his seat in the dining tent and wandered the few yards over to join them. He nodded at the six marines he had requested to accompany them, knowing that adding the four additional armed men would be a cause for some raised eyebrows. But the bridge was the control center for the whole ship, and that meant anything could happen. "Forewarned is forearmed," he said to himself, and then he shook his head. "That was a terrible axiom to use. There must be a better one," he said to himself as he rounded the corner of a side tent, and in front of him was a group of people, all arguing.

"Bullshit—this is bullshit," Ned Beedles yelled. "We need marines on this whole tour like we need a hole in our heads," he finished off.

Professor Cheryl Scholes was nodding, but she didn't say anything. Professor Vincent was yelling back at —more than loud enough for them all.

"It is not bullshit to be aptly prepared—which is what the marines give us. The ability, should the need arise, to defend not us as much as the ship and its technology is the valid reason that they're here today," he said, his voice lower now. Reynolds could tell that he too was upset but not as much as Beedles.

"And what—we now need six of these thick-necked goons—how is that protecting technology?" Beedles yelled.

Boxer, the medical doctor on the team, tried to hold up his hands to stop the back and forth as he shouted, "Wait a minute, wait a minute," but his efforts failed.

"Enough," Reynolds barked at them all and punctuated that with "Sergeant, the next xeno team member that speaks I want you to stun—full stun, if you please," and that threat got through to them all.

Beedles took a step back and was about to speak,

but he thought better of it and closed his mouth.

Reynolds smiled at them all.

Reynolds smiled at them all, and he looked each one in the eyes before he spoke again. "I have asked the marines to add the four new bodies for my own peace of mind. This has nothing to do with you or your thought or even your opinions. I have been charged with the duty—by the Baroness—to tour the bridge and then make my report. The marines—all six of them—are there for my safety, but the idea too that they will protect the Praix technology too is also comforting. Enough. If you wish to stay behind, then do so, but lead us on, please," he said to the marine sergeant, and the soldier went up the ramp into the ship.

Finding walkway number one was easy enough, and they turned to the left to go the hundreds of yards all the way to the bridge that lay well forward. As they walked, Reynolds made sure they were spaced out and the Issian Apostle Jelinek was just ahead of the Praix. He gently sent out the reminder to Jelinek that the Praix must walk with them along with the request to keep him apprised of that so that he'd not simply fly off. That would earn him a marine stun for sure, and moments after he sent that thought to Jelinek, he looked back and got a nod in reply.

After crossing many walkway intersections, they

reached the anteroom that lay just outside the bridge. There, he ensured that the marines opened the door—trying to stay at least one step ahead of the Praix. *No sense in letting the ship know that there is a Praix on the bridge,* he thought.

He went through the door like the rest of the team, and they all stood around the captain's chair —if in fact that was what it was. So he asked that first and got the response he wanted—and more— from the Issian.

"Yes, the chair is for the captain, but it is a slightly older model than our Praix captive knows personally. He explained that in the very previous millennia, there was a need back then since the control of the bridge functions was done by a physical analog methodology. Now, he admitted, their AI was so much more advanced that there were protections on thought commands that didn't exist back then."

"Thought commands? Could we get an explanation of that, please, first?" Reynolds asked.

Jelinek nodded, turned to the Praix, and in a few minutes turned back. "Care and control of any kind of bridge functionality demands that a button be pushed in your human world. We don't do that anymore—we simply think to our ship's AI what we want to happen, and it is carried out by the AI for us. Thought commands are what we call it in

198

SagD.

"But, as he explained, this is an older ship—so there are few thought commands that the AI here can understand and carry out. Buttons need to be pushed here too for everything from changing the temperature of this room to blasting off to outer space. At least that's what he just said to me—well, thought to me," she said.

Reynolds paused to think about that and asked the xeno team for any questions.

Beedles jumped at that chance. "So, if the ship's AI can handle 'some' thought commands—what are they? And we need a list, too ..." he said.

Scholes nodded and filled in what some had obviously been thinking. "And, as he may ask the AI to start up the engines or fill the bridge with poison gas, that might be pretty important, eh?" she added.

Reynolds nodded and the Issian once more turned to the Praix and then back to them all. "He says the commands are basics—housekeeping almost is what he said. But most are down in engineering—where the ship's crew would take control of their engines. Basics like 'rev up to x' or 'close down thrusters' type of items. All the working very rudimentary thought controls were there—there are none here, he says, on the bridge. All here were analog buttons and keyboard entry controls. Remember," he added, "that this ship is twenty-plus thousand years old ..."

That got nods too.

Beedles asked another question. "How is it possible to build a ship that can still operate some twenty-plus thousand years later?"

The Issian answered that one right away. "Because they stole technology from every race that they conquered—and this we know to be true," she answered.

Reynolds nodded but kept to himself the realization that what he'd just learned might be interesting—very, very interesting to the Baroness. He knew this ship had limited AI thought command capabilities, but the newly captured Praix ship—the *Wisp* he had heard it called—had fully functional and modern AI. AI that might, if properly investigated, provide the Barony with the abilities themselves. *Technology that might be taken for our own advantages*, he thought.

As the group went over to the two front chairs, they asked more questions and got answers that seemed to be honest and forthright, at least to Reynolds.

They also went through the whole wall of those cabinets by opening up each cabinet and having their captive look inside to let them know what things were or did. He only knew what few of them were, and they all appeared to be environmental controls here in the ship. Air. Temperature. Air flow. Hydroponics. Water. Many, he said—rather Jelinek said on his behalf—he didn't know nor recognize.

As they moved back to the captain's chair, the Issian stopped them and spoke up, her voice just a bit edgy. "He wants to know if he could take the captain's perch? He says that just his DNA on that perch will power up the whole of the bridge—and he reminded me that the engines are wrecked and that there would be no repercussions from this. He did say it wasn't for his benefit at all … just if you wanted to see things as they should be.

All the xeno team looked at Reynolds.

So it comes down to this—and the choice is all mine, Reynolds thought. He looked away for a second and then decided. "Marines, please circle the captain's chair—sorry, captain's perch. Xeno team step back, please, and Apostle, yes, have him step up there. Marines, if you detect anything untoward, full stun in an instant, if you please!" he said forcefully. Maybe more forcefully than what was needed as he remembered that the Praix couldn't hear or understand him.

But he did remember to ask Jelinek to repeat his commands to the Praix, who stepped up to the perch and then grabbed the bar with the talons of both feet.

Moments later, the lighting in the room changed; it become more mellow, Reynolds thought, if he had to pick a word.

The forward area of the bulkhead that was black suddenly changed to a backlit view-screen like on any bridge of any ship. The scene was a hodgepodge of rocky jumbled colors and swirls. The Praix didn't ask, but he leaned down with his beak and clicked so quickly on the console that there was no time to stop him—and the view-screen suddenly showed being airborne over Ghayth. The ship was flying along over a huge set of rocky mountains, most covered in snow, and the peaks were amazing.

The marines had all drawn their stunners, but with a gesture from Reynolds, they now lowered them o but kept them in hand in case something else might occur.

The view-screen continued to show the Ghayth terrain as though the ship continued flying, but Reynolds looked around the bridge instead of only at the screen. There was a new bank of machinery, but when he looked closer, he realized it was a hologram against the near wall. It looked like there were many controls, and he wondered if one could actually click one of them to control whatever functionality it might control. He had no idea. But he was glad there was going to be a video of all of this, and he wondered if it might give more answers to what he'd just experienced.

He looked down at the monitor at the captain's perch and noted which icons were now lit up and brand new to see, and he made sure that his vid included that too.

As he looked behind him later, when they were all leaving the bridge, the lighting changed, the captain's perch monitor went back to all grayed-out icons and the holographic bank of machines disappeared. *Only works when a Praix is in the chair —or perch,* he thought.

That was a new truth too ... so much to try to digest and then write that report for the Baroness ...

CHAPTER SEVEN

The thing that woke him, Bram thought, was the worst thing any navy man wanted to hear—a screaming klaxon though it was not as loud as it could have been. As he rolled over in his bunk, he realized that the klaxon was not going off on his ship, the *Crimson I*, but it was outside all over the landing port. It was still loud. And, from what he could tell, there more than one klaxon was going off.

He got up on one elbow and said, "AI, put the landing field exterior view on my view-screen."

A second later, the view-screen filled with the view from the landing port. *Something is definitely up*, he thought.

The entire field was lit up with huge lights and searchlights were beaming up into the still dark sky.

He had no idea what time it was, but that much of a commotion out there was not a good sign. He sighed, slid out of the bunk and the warm duvet, and put his feet down on bare cool deck. That woke him up, and he shook his head.

"AI, whatever the issue is out there, connect me to the Oirus landing admin channel. Send through a request about this commotion."

Moments later, on the view-screen, text began to crawl along the bottom of the view-screen:

Security warning. Security warning. The Noriega destroyer NN Paladin is landing.
Please escalate your own vessel's security to its maximum …
Security warning. Security warning.
The Noriega destroyer NN Paladin is landing.
Please escalate your own vessel's security to its maximum …

He read that and wondered what it really meant. He messaged his bridge and ordered the duty officer to button up the *Crimson I*, and then he wondered why he'd done that. The ship was clad in Xithricite, so it was invulnerable, but these Warlord space realms didn't know that as yet. Still, best to follow suit.

He sat and watched, and in twenty more minutes, the destroyer came down on her Inertial Drive and slowly lowered herself. Shortly thereafter, she sat

on her landing fins and settled on the assigned pad.
And then nothing happened. Not a single ramp
came down nor did the big landing escalator extend
itself either. But those damn klaxons were turned
off at least.

Bram said, "AI, can you please get me info on
this Noriega warlord, please," and in a minute, the
sidebar began to scroll down with that information.
He read and then he paused the scrolling. Then he
started it once more and read to the end.

Noriega was the name of the warlord himself,
and as the custom here was, it was also the name of
the group of planets that had been seized by the
Warlord too. It was the same as the Tunander
Coalition with their dictator named Tunander.

But there was more. It seemed that the Noriega
group was in what couldn't be called anything else
but a battle to be the biggest dictatorship in Warlord
space, and that war was with Konoe.

Noriega had six planets, and Konoe had ten.
Noriega was trying to expand by any means
necessary to become bigger than Konoe. At least
that's what Gallipedia reported, and Bram did see
the sense of that. He did not understand the lengths
to which they would go to achieve those goals, but
he knew the "expand or die" values were shared by
many species both on and off the RIM. The Praix
alone were an example of a species who lived and

breathed that edict.

Further, he read, the dictator Noriega had been a senior minister in the old Pentyaan Oligarchy, and his area of specialty was in economics. What that had to do with being a dictator, Bram didn't have any idea, but he did know one thing. The klaxons had woken him, and that was a good thing. *Wonder what will happen if—*

The AI sounded three beeps and he stopped that thinking immediately.

"Here we go," he said to himself.

"Captain, you have an incoming EYES ONLY message from one Sithe Ogrunder of the Tunander Coalition who requests that you pick up immediately. Do you have an answer for me to reply to the sender, Captain?"

He sat for a whole minute. *This needs more back story than what I can handle now in the middle of the night. That and I need to be in the game but from a position of more strength than wakened by klaxons in the middle of the night.*

"AI, please send this answer," he said as he composed his thoughts. "Your message was received, but as it is the middle of the night, it was held. In the morning, it will be given to the captain of the *Crimson I* at ten hundred hours."

Bram sighed. "Send that verbatim, AI. Then close the Ansible, and do not accept any more messages until that time tomorrow. Confirm."

And a moment later, the *Crimson I* AI said, "Confirmed, Captain, and good night," and the speakers went quiet.

He turned off the view-screen and then rearranged the duvet covering him. "Tomorrow might be a very interesting day," he said to himself. "Very interesting indeed ..."

#####

More than a decade ago when mind linking was brand new to him, it used to hit him like a freight train. Now he knew what to expect as he suddenly fell down that big dark hole—a shaft that seemed to go on and on forever. Of course, now, after hundreds of these mind links, he knew what would happen next.

He looked down at the center of the black hole and, yes, there was a pinpoint of light. He didn't bother anymore to try to swim toward that light or guide himself there; instead he just watched the pinpoint grow in size. Eventually, it became a brighter larger ball of light. And still the light grew until it was all around him as the blackness receded above his head.

And he heard the whisper now too. With a group mind link, there were many whispers, each from one of the brains in the group, but this time, there was only one whisper from the Master Adept's mind. And the Master Adept appeared directly in front of him as the whiteness around him snapped out of existence and his quarters appeared to his now working eyes.

It was morning, and he'd just woken up. Somehow, in his sleep, he had made the assumption that the only thing to do was to ask for help—that was what the Master Adept in his dreams had said to him.

So now, he was here, mind linked to the Master Adept in person—and he was tongue-tied. He didn't know what to say or how to even approach the way he felt. Perhaps he was in over his head. He felt like a straw man in the captain's chair. He felt so far out of his depth that he really had no idea how to say any of this to the Master Adept.

So he sat, opened up his hands, palms up, and simply said, "Help ... I need help, Master ..."

She looked at him, and as always, she was dressed exactly the same as always. She wore her brown robe with the cowl neck and hanging from a chain around her neck was the big Issian medallion with the icon, the ringed planet of Eons, on her chest.

She did not smile at him at all. She just stared at the face of the man in front of her. Not a single emotion seemed to be on her face, and that never changed. One hand was curled up in her lap, and the other was on that ringed planet medallion on her chest, stroking the edge with a nail.

As he looked at her, he felt her slowly inserting her mind's tendrils within his own. He didn't fight back; he simply sat wide open and waited. He knew that she would see quickly how he felt. Why he felt that way would take more time. But eventually, he knew she would speak when she had an idea of the problem—and how she might help.

She nodded to him then, and inside his head, it felt like those mind reading tendrils were slowly drifting away. She picked up a cup of tea, had a sip, and then put it down.

"Bram, so good to have you visit with me this morning—well, it is later afternoon here on Eons. I see that you have some issues, and that is good. A captain must always find ways to balance the various factors in front of him—to make a valid and knowledgeable choice."

She sipped again from her tea, and this time she must have finished the cup as Bram saw her nod to someone beside her, to get a refill, he assumed.

"That, and yes, there is this whole new Noriega situation—which I do not know about as you do not know either. But I do have these words for you," she said, and she leaned forward just a bit when she spoke to him again.

"You need to forget that you're new to the captaincy—you are the one there in charge. You must take charge, Bram—you are the RIM Confederacy to these warlords. Confidence is what you need, and while that usually comes only from experience, you will remember that I have the ability to look ahead. To see the future of some people is a gift—one that I have in strength," she said, and again, she took a moment to have more tea.

He nodded. He wanted to know right now what his future looked like.

She smiled then. "What I see is that you are at the crux of a major change that will be happening in the future of the RIM Confederacy—and Warlord space. I will not comment on the choices that you will face, but I know that you make the right moves in each case—that I can see. You have the word of your own Master Adept, Bram," she said, and a nod was now added to that smile.

The relief he felt was like a wave of warm air on a cold night. He'd make choices, yes, but he now knew those choices were going to be the right ones. Just knowing that was so much of a confidence builder that he slapped his knee and almost laughed right out loud.

He nodded to the Master Adept, and he thanked

her profusely for her help and, of course, for taking the time to help a new captain. The mind link was broken, and he was once more alone in his quarters.

On Eons, in her quarters, the Master Adept sipped her tea yet again. By telling such a lie to Bram, she might have endangered his mission, but that was not why she'd done that. Giving the young man the strength to be the captain and make decisions was the reason she had lied.

And that was a good thing … at least I hope so, and she took yet another sip of tea.

#####

The meeting was held—at the insistence of Tunander himself, Sithe Ogrunder told Bram as he finally took last night's EYES ONLY request—at a few minutes past ten hundred hours. It was a simple message, and it had an update on it as well.

The Noriega head of state—Noriega himself, it appeared—requested a meeting with both the RIM Confederacy representatives and the Tunander representatives. He had requested this happen in the middle of last night, but that had been a moot point since Bram hadn't taken the call.

And then there was the update. Just two hours ago, Ogrunder had updated the message to add that the meeting would be fine with the Tunander side and that the dictator himself would be at the meeting, which was now going to be at noon in the administration building on the landing port. Ogrunder had added that they had refused to meet on the *Paladin* and insisted the meeting was on neutral soil. The administration building on the landing port had also been chosen as the Noriega side had refused to go to the official residence for the Tunander with the big arched building and those huge stairs.

Bram said to himself, "Neutral territory maybe for them, but not so much for us." He acknowledged his receipt and reading of the message and replied that, yes, the RIM Confederacy diplomats would attend that luncheon meeting. The message went out immediately.

He grinned for a second to himself, wondering if he had gone a bit too far with his luncheon modifier, but he thought it might calm things down at a meeting that was going to be a doozy. While he'd never heard the word doozy growing up on Eons, he had heard it at the naval academy, and it described a course to not take as it was too hard and too demanding.

He sighed. *This one is gonna be a real doozy.* He went to his keyboard and once more dialed in for Gallipedia and asked for more information on Noriega and Konoe. As he read, he wondered how hungry each was when it came to expansion since there was little information on that rationale. But it really didn't matter; after all, no matter what happened at the meeting, he could not make a mistake, he reminded himself. *My karma train has come in—thanks to the Master Adept,* he thought, and he couldn't quite shake the smug feeling knowing that gave him.

He showered. He had his steward put a fresh press on a set of dress whites, liking the duke's choice of the plain color as well as how crisp the uniform looked. He looked himself over in the big mirror on the back of the closet door in his quarters. "AI, notify the ambassador that I'll meet him down on the landing deck in ten," he said.

He picked up his tablet and made some modifications to the automatic settings. From now on, the tablet would record the audio and its camera would save everything that happened in front of the tablet too.

Done. I look good. All is prepared. I am ready for this meeting, he thought and left his quarters to take the lift down to Deck One.

Minutes later, he stood on the deck, looking out across the landing port at the ship from Noriega, the *Paladin.* She sat almost twenty landing pads from the *Crimson I,* all alone way out at the far end of the landing port. In front of her sat a small carrier vehicle, for transport over to the administration building, with two guards standing in front of same.

As he looked down again, he noted there was a similar vehicle waiting in front of the *Crimson I*.

"Morning, Captain," a voice said from behind him, and as he turned, Ambassador Harmon smiled and offered his hand.

Bram shook his hand. "You clean up very nicely, Ambassador," he said, and he was right.

The ambassador wore the dress blues of the RIM Confederacy, and it was less of a military uniform than one might think. There were no ribbons on his chest and no epaulettes on his shoulders. There were some badges of service on his chest instead. There were ten gold stripes on his left sleeve. Each represented five years of service in the RIM Confederacy Diplomatic Corps, and if that meant anything to anyone anywhere, it had to be an important factor in judging the man himself.

After shaking hands, they walked down the long ramp to the tarmac toward the waiting vehicle.

As they reached it, one of the Tunander guards, who was taking a call from someone, held up his hand to delay the two of them.

Bram was only slightly perturbed, but then the grinding roar of a landing ramp being extended hit them. He turned, like they all did, and over at the

Paladin, he saw the lower deck on the destroyer was extending outward. In a minute, it hit the tarmac, and down the ramp came a vehicle—a small personnel carrier—that went right by the waiting Tunander Coalition vehicle and its two guards and sped toward the administration building.

The guard gestured toward them and said, "Please board, Captain," as he moved out of the way.

"What was that?" Ambassador Harmon asked.

"The Noriega didn't need our ride, I suspect," the guard said, and Bram heard a little sarcasm in the guard's tone.

The vehicle followed the personnel carrier, and in a minute, both arrived at the front of the administration building. Bram got out quickly and was followed by the ambassador, but they noted the vehicle from the other ship was already empty. They had only been there a half a minute, but the passengers—whomever they were—were already inside.

The Tunander Coalition guards led them up the stairs, and they went into the building, turned to the left, and walked down a short hall to a room.

Bram had expected a meeting room, but that was not what they had been taken to. Instead, they had reached the building's cafeteria. It was full of tables and chairs and had a complete serving line on the far side. More than a dozen servers stood behind the serving line with its long metal rails for sliding food trays. *Strange, but they are all watching the guests come in,* Bram thought as he turned to his left and stopped cold.

The first time he had met Tunander, he had thought the man was dressed like a "banana republic" dictator, but the attire of the three men from the *Paladin* far surpassed Tunander's.

Each was a human—or appeared to be a human —of about six feet in height. Each wore an identical khaki uniform. But the uniform was completely without any kind of normal badging.

Across the chest was a band of olive green. On it were small star-shaped patches in rows. One man had several of those patches—many more than the other two. *Must be the one in charge,* Bram thought. The three men from the *Paladin* stood there looking at Bram and Ambassador Harmon.

Bram made the first move and stepped forward. "I'm Captain Bram Sander of the *Crimson I*—the big red ship out there. And this is Ambassador Harmon, and we're both from the RIM Confederacy on a diplomatic call to the Tunander Coalition."

He smiled and he waited. None of the three men opposite him said anything for several seconds, but eventually, the man with the most patches nodded and stepped forward.

"I am Noriega. I ordered this meeting. Where is the Tunander?" he said.

Rude, Bram thought and mentally shook his head, but he said nothing.

From behind him, the head of state of the Tunander Coalition spoke up. "As usual, Noriega, you are being rude to our guests—not your guests. But yes, let's get this whole thing started, shall we?" He turned then and walked over to a table that had been set for nine guests, and everyone followed. He smiled at Bram and Ambassador Harmon and said, "I think perhaps we should eat first and then talk —"

"No. We are not here to eat. We are here to listen to your excuses," Noriega said and sat. One of his aides sat to his left and the other on his right.

Tunander nodded, turned to Bram, and gestured over to the cafeteria line. Bram didn't smile too much, but he led the way over to the line. He took a tray, put some silverware on it, moved to the rails, and put the tray down. He looked at the first lady behind the line and said, "What's good today?"

She smiled at him as she stepped forward and pointed at the various compartments behind the clear glass. "Sir, we have a wide selection of some of the planet's best-known and loved dishes. Here, we have our appetizers—everything from fresh, raw rodent to fish to a platter that has a large selection to choose from, if you prefer."

As she spoke, Bram looked down to see what looked like a six-legged varmint of some kind staring back at him. "Probably pickled," he said to himself, but the gentle tremor up his back reminded him that he wouldn't touch that at all. Ever.

He nodded and said, "And then?" He moved his tray down the line a few feet.

The same person followed him to show him the entrées, the sides, soups, salads, and eventually desserts.

He ended up selecting a small portion of some kind of fish fillet. *Looks odd, but it is cooked and does smell good,* he thought. He then chose something steamed that reminded him of rice. And for dessert, he chose a piece of what the lady behind the line had said was a fruit pie.

He sat and a moment later, the ambassador returned to the table with a full tray, laden with food. Bram raised an eyebrow, which the ambassador noticed, and he whispered, "Bram, it is always good to eat well."

Across the table and down a few chairs, Noriega sat and watched them.

Mad. The guy is pretty mad, which is a good thing, Bram thought. *One can sometimes use that anger to get someone to make a judgment call and action based on that anger. And in negotiations, using a man's anger against him is often a bonus.*

Tunander came back to the table with a large portion of the same fish Bram had. Once he was seated, he said to Noriega, "Perhaps as we eat, you can tell us why you wanted this meeting."

Not polite. Not perhaps really necessary from one head of state to another, Bram thought. Still, Bram saw, it did make Noriega blanch a little more.

Noriega nodded, and it looked like he tried to curb his tongue. "Tunander, your coalition was the place that the RIM Confederacy came. We want to know why. And more than that, we want you to remember that your coalition is a part of the Warlord space—a full partner," he said forcefully.

Tunander smiled as he speared a large piece of fish on his fork and gently placed it in his mouth. He chewed. One didn't talk when one chewed, so they waited. Bram tried that rice-like dish, and it wasn't bad at all. It was steamed and the small kernels had a spongy inside with a brittle cover around it. Bram thought it tasted a bit fishy, but that might have been from the fish fillet sitting beside it on the same plate.

Tunander swallowed and then spoke slowly and softly but firmly. "Noriega. We didn't move the planet to visit them—the RIM showed up here. Why? We don't know. We have been hospitable

hosts though. We took them on a tour of all four of
our worlds in one day. We have our holidays,
which end this evening with the big festival. And
tomorrow, I will sit with the captain and his
ambassador to talk about the reason for their visit.
But I'm sure—positive, in fact—that this has
nothing to do with you or your space, Noriega." He
didn't smile. He just looked at the dictator across
the table from him.

Noriega jumped to his feet, pointing a finger at
Tunander, and his voice went up in volume until he
was shouting. "I know there's another reason, and
don't think that I won't find it either. You are on
notice from the Warlord space that we will be
watching. And at the first sign of any double-
dealing or treachery, the whole might of the three of
us warlords will come down on you—both of you,"
he said, spittle flying out of his lips as he was so
mad. He stormed off, followed by his two sidekicks.

Bram wondered if they'd even ask the landing
authority for permission to leave or just jump up
and off planet on their own. He took another bite of
the fish and decided that he did like it. He ate
slowly and in a few minutes more, he was done.

He tried the pie last, but he didn't like it. If it was
Oirus fruit, then he'd hate to see the tree it was
grown on as he thought it tasted like a mix between
mud and soot.

Tunander watched him finish and then smiled. "Noriega is more than incorrect in that we—you and I have no hidden agenda. We haven't even talked as yet. But, that will happen soon if that'd be okay with you—and you too, Ambassador?"

Bram bowed his head, smiled, and said, "At your convenience, Tunander. Just let us know where and when."

The lunch broke up, and instead of taking the carrier back to the *Crimson I*, Ambassador Harmon and Bram decided to walk. They talked and decided that tomorrow they would be honest and forthright with Tunander, but they would keep the Jannah request on the down low.

Bram smiled at that, as the whole situation was going to get a lot more complicated when the Caliph and Baroness each sent negotiation teams to visit Jannah.

The ready room on the *Gibraltar* was large, yet for Admiral Vennamo to receive the Baroness and then offer refreshments and hold a meeting, it was a bit cramped. *Maybe not for myself and the Baroness, but then there were the inevitable EliteGuards, the hangers-on like aides ... How many chairs should I even have the stewards set up?*

She stood and threw up her hands. "Ten. Put

eight chairs over against the bulkhead there," she said as she pointed toward an inner wall. "And then the two here opposite my own seat at the captain's console."

Stewards jumped and reset the chairs according to the admiral's wishes. One came forward and said, "Admiral, will this do?"

The eight chairs were in a line against the inner wall that separated the ready room from the bridge. Against the exterior bulkhead, the view-screen showed Neres below, in all its daylight glory. Next was the captain's console with her chair against the desk side and the two chairs opposite her chair. A small cart that carried pastries, tea, coffee, and even wine had been wheeled in. Her chief steward had prompted her that sometimes the Baroness looked for wine, and as it was almost noon, Eleanor had okayed the addition of a small selection of Quaran whites. She hoped that this would not be seen as being improper; one might think it odd, but then again, pleasing a Royal was sometimes a guessing game.

She sat in her chair, looked at her monitor, and noted that the inbound shuttle from Neres City, carrying the Baroness, was on time and should dock on the *Gibraltar* in less than ten minutes.

The reason for the visit was still an unknown. There had just been a notice to expect the Baroness on this date at this time. "Maybe I'm getting my walking papers—she's found someone else to be the Barony Navy admiral. Or maybe she's going to resign and … never mind," she said to herself, "I'll know in a few minutes." She stood and went through the door connecting the ready room with the *Gibraltar* bridge.

"Admiral on the bridge," her XO barked out, and as usual, she waved it off.

"Yes, XO, thank you. The Baroness is coming aboard, and you will give her all the deference a Royal deserves. She will pass right through the bridge to meet with me in my ready room. I do not know how long our meeting will last, but you all had better look busy, busy when she's on the bridge. That understood?" she asked.

The "Wilcos" rang out, and that handled that problem. She smiled at them all and then went out of the bridge to wait in the corridor where the Baroness would be coming along soon. In less than five minutes, she heard the tramp of the EliteGuards' measured walk coming around the curved corridor first. Moments later, the Baroness came into view and she was smiling.

"Good sign," Eleanor said to herself, and she walked forward to meet the head of state of the Barony.

"Baroness, so good to see you—hopefully the

shuttle ride up was fine?" she asked, thinking that small talk was always a good starter.

"It was fine, Admiral, and the pilot gave us a full sweep around the *Gibraltar* too. The ship looks very good, and that is a reflection of the person in charge —so kudos to you, Admiral." She smiled as they entered the bridge and was able to look surprised when the XO stated, "Baroness on the bridge," and the bridge crew jumped to their feet with small bows.

She looked happy at that and said, "Please as you all were, nice to be on the *Gibraltar*." She walked right by them on her way to the ready room.

"Starts with a compliment and then all to business—traditional characteristics," the admiral said to herself.

The Baroness went right over to the refreshments, and shooing away a steward, she poured her own tea. She did look over the pastries and chose a raisin tart. No wine. No coffee. None of the little doughnuts or Danishes either. All she chose to go with her tea was a raisin tart in its little foil shell.

She sat alone opposite the admiral's chair, and the admiral noticed they were alone in the ready room. She had brought no aides—and the EliteGuards were still out in the bridge. *Probably just eying the crew,* she thought as she poured herself a cup of coffee and then sat carefully at her console.

"Hope the refreshments are fine, Ma'am?" *Best to stick with more small talk and let the Baroness get to the point when she wants,* Admiral Vennamo thought.

The Baroness nodded as she had taken a bite of the raisin tart and smiled as she chewed. "I am especially fond of these ones, so yes, they're fine, Admiral."

No movement to the point of the meeting as yet, so Eleanor smiled back at her and took a bite of the cherry Danish that she had picked. She chewed slowly hoping they'd move along past small talk soon.

"You know, Admiral, that I asked for this meeting, correct? I mean, your aides told you that as well as that I requested that the *Gibraltar* be ready for a trip off the RIM, correct?"

The admiral was blindsided. No one had told her that at all. But as always, she was ready for anything.

"Yes, Ma'am. We're ready for any kind of mission to anywhere, Ma'am," she said. *Almost true too,* she thought.

"Well, here's what I need done—a sort of '"undercover" type of mission. One thing to show everyone else, yet a hidden agenda for you to act upon ..."

She went on for almost a full half hour on the

mission of the *Crimson I*. She explained about the agreements between the Caliph, the Duke d'Avigdor, and herand that she had donated the *Defiant* to the mission. She explained that Bram Sander, an Issian and a past Adept Officer, had been promoted to full captaincy of the *Crimson I* by the duke and that he was charged with the duty to find opportunities for the RIM Confederacy to grow by seeking out realms that might be interested in joining the Confederacy. And he had done just that. Out in Warlord space—the new name for the failed Pentyaan Oligarchy—there was just such a group—the Tunander Coalition. And one of their planets was interested in joining the RIM, but it had no real position on whether to join as a full member or as a realm of a current member

"And that is why I am here today," the Baroness said. "What I want to happen is to send you and the *Gibraltar* to this Tunander Coalition to talk to this interested planet, Jannah, I believe it's called. You will present to them a full proposal to join the Barony, and I give you all the opportunity to get them aboard. You may let them know that as a member of the RIM Confederacy, they would receive the Barony Drive too. Either as a full member or as a subordinate realm to a full member. That may also be a real chip to play with their dictator too—offer up to, say, five Barony Drive units if a price needs to be paid to buy the Jannah world," she said, sipping her tea once again.

"But that's the public face that you will present. There is another that you will keep confidential. And it's this," she said as she took another bite of the tart and finished it off. "What I want you to be more aware of are the other realms that are in this coalition. I understand that there are four—of which Jannah is the only stated one looking for a change. But there will be others watching and noting it all—and it's those ones that I want to know about. Who they are. What they might be looking for. What might get them to 'buy in' to the Barony. That's your real job on this mission, Eleanor—are you up for it?"

She replied immediately, "Of course, Baroness. We will look one way but have our ears to the ground for all other opportunities, Ma'am." She felt this was going to be a difficult task but one she could handle.

The Baroness nodded and went on about the other items she would need to be aware of too. The Caliph was also sending a team to make their own proposal to the Jannah representatives. Since the duke had passed on this opportunity, there were only going to be the two offers to Jannah.

I wonder why that is, the admiral thought. *For the duke to just decline an opportunity to add another realm to the Duchy d'Avigdor was an odd thing to do.* She wondered if there was more to this than could be seen, and she'd ensure she remained aware of this and watchful.

The Baroness smiled at her admiral. "Eleanor, I know you. I know your skills and talent. This mission is perfect for you—and I know that you'll come back with some solid information too. Best of luck—you need to be in Tunander by the day after tomorrow. Please, keep me in the loop, as the younger set says." She sipped the end of her tea and rose quickly.

The admiral was on her feet a second later, and as they left the ready room, the EliteGuards fell into line behind them. They went out of the bridge to the corridor beyond.

"I can find my own way back to the shuttle, Admiral—and I'd think that you have preparations to get done. Good luck, Admiral," the Baroness said over her shoulder as she went down the curved corridor toward the lift down to the landing bay deck.

The admiral went back to her ready room and sat after taking another cherry Danish. A simple proposal to make to the Jannah representatives was the easy part. Watching the others in the Tunander Coalition as much as possible was the harder part of the task. And the Caliph's team would be just as eager to gain a new realm as she was.

She chewed a large bite of the Danish, enjoying the taste and drank some of the sweet coffee to wash it down. ""Time—well, in ten minutes maybe —to get organized and ready for the trip to Warlord space ..." she said to herself.

CHAPTER EIGHT

"Sir, we have established the one system that the RIM ship appears to be coming from, Sir. And it's system R17, Sir," the helmsman on the *Paladin* said. His voice as always was very deferential, and as always, he was very militarily polite. On the bridge of the destroyer, his captain and the man who ran the Noriega group of planets, the dictator Noriega, sat behind him. But as per orders, when the dictator was on the bridge, he was the one that all were to respond to.

Noriega nodded and turned to the captain. "And how much should we trust this, Captain?" he asked.

Seated in the chair reserved for him alone, in his plain khaki uniform with all those patches, he took another big bite of the sandwich a steward had brought to the bridge on a tray. He'd helped himself after which the rest of the bridge crew had waited until he told them to go ahead. It was a triple decker sandwich with layers of bread, meat, cheese, and big ripe slices of a purple pepper.

"Sir, I believe that we can at least trust the veracity of the decision that it must be R17. We've spent more than five weeks off Memories, watching the ship appear from inside Warlord space. And while we can't track their Barony Drive like we can scan for our own TachyonDrive—it looks like that is the system, Sir. Will take a couple of days to get there, but should be fruitful, Sir."

"Better be, Captain. Or else," Noriega said between chews, and he gulped down his bottled juice. He looked up at the view-screen on the bridge wall and said, "Plot a course to this R17 system— sidebar with details."

The XO behind the captain complied immediately. The system appeared. It had a normal G3 sun with seven planets in orbit. Two of same, the sidebar on the view-screen noted, were in the Goldilocks zone where life could occur. According to Gallipedia, there was life on both—but no sentient life. One of the two had no moons, but the other, inward or closer to the sun itself, had a moon and a ring of asteroids as well in the same lunar orbit but not much more.

The captain read the information on the sidebar as the rest of the bridge did, and he wondered if that was at all important. The RIM ship, a frigate, came out of this system once a week now and would arrive at Memories. Then a half hour later, it yawed and jumped, using its Barony Drive, out of Warlord space and into the RIM Confederacy. Five times, they'd had a frigate there too, watching, and all five times they'd made calculations by hand as they used to in the old days to try to determine where the frigate had come from. And R17 seemed to be the place.

"With your permission, Sir," the captain said, "I'll have the helm take us to R17 for a look-see? As it's not within any real Warlord realms—it's plain free space, Sir, so there is no reason not to go, realm-wise, Sir."

The captain wouldn't, of course, ever just have done that on his own. He had to ask. He wondered if his peers would think that having the captaincy of the *Paladin*, which meant not being able to do anything, was a great career move. But then he didn't much care. With more ships in the Noriega group than any other Warlord had, he was happy to have a captaincy, but he so hoped that the dictator wouldn't be along on more missions.

"Without a doubt, Captain—make it so. And it is still within the old Pentyaan Oligarchy space, so it

is our own area to explore and to keep out any
intruders too. That is a fact, Captain," the man
beside him said between bites of his big sandwich.
"And, Captain, I want on my tablet—before the end
of today—a plan on what we should do when we
get there. Search? Fight? I want your options—best-
case and worst-case options too," he said.

The captain said, "Wilco, Sir," and he got to
work on his console and tried to ignore the loud
chewing sounds from a few feet away.

The *CN Roc* popped into normal space in low
orbit over Tunander in the middle of the afternoon
and was immediately challenged by the landing
port authority. On the bridge, the man in the
captain's chair was Admiral Magnusson, who
nodded to his Ansible officer, and the ship was
granted landing access down to the planet's landing
port. Moments later, the destroyer was going down
to the landing port and had been assigned a landing
pad close to the *Crimson I*.

"Ignore it," Magnusson said as his Ansible officer
was beginning to turn to let him know the *Crimson
I* was trying to contact them.

The Ansible officer replied, "Wilco," and the ship
continued to go down tail first. The landing took all
of nine minutes, and as she settled, there was

another chime from the Ansible, and once again, his officer turned toward him. "Sir, it's the *Crimson I* again—they want us to know that we're expected to come over for a meeting ASAP?"

As she looked at him, and he realized he had no idea what her name was, but that was because as a brand new admiral, he still hadn't as yet chosen his own bridge crew. He smiled at her. "Officer ..." he said, looking at her.

"Sir, I'm Lieutenant Gould—Ansible officer first class with my certs all done and accredited for, Sir," she said.

There was pride in her voice, and he heard that loud and clear. He also knew that to be certified in the Ansible order was a difficult task with more work than reward.

He nodded to her. "Here's what I'd like to say on that—for the whole bridge to listen to, if you all please," he said, and everyone stopped working except the officer at the helm who was closing down ship-wide systems.

"We represent the Caliphate Navy here. So we are an entity unto ourselves. We will most likely work with the duchy on the *Crimson I* and even the Baroness's team when they get here. But we answer to no one. Polite, military protocols—but no obeying any kind of orders. From anyone. Got that?"

In unison, the bridge crew responded, "Wilco, Sir."

"Lieutenant Gould—notify the *Crimson I* that we've just arrived and are settling in. But that in a couple of hours, if they would like to come over for a visit, we'd be glad to have them as guests." His look was one of calm collected leadership—at least he hoped it was.

His Ansible lieutenant did her job, and in moments, she looked back at her admiral. "Sir, they will be here in one hour—and I was told to tell you that it is Captain Sander who will be here, the leader of the RIM Confederacy mission to Warlord space, Sir," she said.

Figures that they'd try to remind me that someone else is the leader here, he thought. *But that was not entirely true—I, as the Caliphate admiral, am in charge of my own realm's mission here. Will have to remind Sander of that.*

After the normal flow of reports and landing routines, there was a chime from the *Roc's* AI.

"Notice that there are visitors on the landing deck, seeking entry to the ship. Three humans identified as Captain Sander, his XO, Rostrum, and Major Stal, a Barony marine. We await their authorizations to allow entry," the AI announced and waited.

Bram and Alver he knew, and the XO was from

the *Scavenger* ship and the Memories battle with the defeated reaper aliens. He knew they'd won that one, but he still had no opinion of her, so there was more to learn.

"Allow them entry, have them escorted up to my ready room here on the bridge," Magnusson said to the AI. He nodded to his XO and said, "Comm to you."

He went over to the door and into the ready room. In a few minutes, the door reopened, and in walked Captain Sander, his XO, and the marine major. They all nodded to him, as he hadn't gotten up from behind his console. They also noted there were only two other chairs. Bram took one and gestured for his XO to sit in the other, and Alver stood at ease behind the chairs.

"You're an admiral now, Magnusson?" Bram said.

Okay, that sets the tone, he thought. "I am an admiral, yes, in the Caliphate Navy—and as only a captain, I would expect you to follow military protocol and to address me as sir. Got that, captain?"

Bram stared at him and then nodded. "Absolutely true, Admiral. My apologies, Sir," he said, his words clipped.

Okay, that's out of the way, Magnusson thought. "You asked to see us, Captain. What can we do you for?"

Bram nodded and then leaned forward. "We have a complete report to tender for your use—it's our mission details over the past few weeks. We expect that the Baroness's team—on the *BN Gibraltar*—will arrive tomorrow. The meeting with the Tunander—he's the local warlord dictator who has the four planets the report covers—will be in three days. Realm-wide holidays have prevented us from getting to that level, but it will happen soon. The Jannah offer is also in the report for your consideration, and as we all know, they will choose from your offer or the Baroness's offer to become a subordinate realm under their membership in the RIM Confederacy."

He stopped then, but Magnusson said nothing.

Bram continued. "There is, however, a 'fly in the ointment,' as they say, and it too is covered in the report, but it's about this other warlord, Noriega. He has called us both—the Tunander and the RIM—out and has stated that he will not allow any kind of dealing between us. Or, we will face the wrath of the other three warlords. Sounds like a threat to me, Admiral. Have you any opinion on that?"

Magnusson looked at Bram and half-smiled. "I do. I think that they have a lot to learn. Anything else?" *Being short and curt seems to be the way to go,* he thought. *The major's stare is a bit over the top, but*

238

then he reports to Sander. Magnusson's smile broadened. "Then thank you. If any more information becomes available, then do let me— rather, let the Caliphate representatives here know," he said.

That got nods from them, and he waited. Eventually, the captain across from him saluted first. Magnusson answered with his own salute, as formal as ever.

#####

"Admiral, we're getting landing pad number eleven, Ma'am," the helmsman said as he'd been instructed to do.

Admiral Vennamo nodded and said, "Fine ... set her down, Lieutenant."

As she watched the planet beneath her slowly spin to port, the *Gibraltar* tipped up so her aft went down first as always. Now, the ship looked out toward the Milky Way galaxy and its huge swath of stars. First lay the big black—as it was called by all —the wide swath with very few stars in it that separated the arm of the galaxy where the RIM lay from the next inner arm. More than three thousand lights the big black was, and it took years to cross it with TachyonDrive engines. It took seconds with the Barony Drive, and she wondered if, in the near future, there would be more trips across the big black just to see what was there or who was there.

She didn't dwell on that, but she did have a small tinge of wistfulness about that idea. She'd love to pilot the *Gibraltar* there herself. *Another time and another realm,* she thought and grinned as she tried to forget about exploring new vistas.

A few minutes later, the *Gibraltar* set down, perfectly too, she thought, and she tried to button up her console but a flashing icon had already appeared on her monitor. She ignored it for a few more minutes as she was signing off on a report, but then she clicked the icon. There was a meeting request with Captain Sander for later that day. *He's a captain now?* she thought. *Boy, things change.* She hit the accept button and then looked after a few more reports, and finally she was done.

Being the Barony admiral did have its perks, she thought as moments later she was entering her quarters. Her quarters were big with three rooms— a bathroom, a bedroom, and a living room She spent more time in the living room area than in any of the other rooms. She dropped her sidearm on the couch and smiled. Even though she wore a stunner, she'd never used it, and now as the admiral, she'd probably never use it in the future either. With all of the guards always around—Provost guards from the ship, marines, and even EliteGuards when there was Royalty aboard—she'd be the last one to draw a weapon. *Probably should drop the wearing of same,* she thought, and she decided that was exactly what she'd do. Picking up the holster, she marched it over to the wall unit and tucked it up high on the topmost shelf. *Done.*

After her shower, she looked at herself in the mirror. *Single, Caucasian female of indeterminate age,* she thought and snickered. She was thirty-nine, but only her personnel file said that. In her youth, her brown hair had been many other colors, but brown suited her now and her hair reached just to her collar. Her eyes were brown too, and she thought her nose was a bit to thin. As she disliked jewelry, she wore no earrings in her ears.

Instead of accessorizing with jewelry, she chose to accessorize with technology. She always had a PDA on—that was her one big addiction. *Always the latest, the best, and the most expensive. That's my mantra,* she thought. It allowed her to be in touch, but she was able to do it with style and flair. Her pupils were dilating, she saw, as she thought about the latest one she'd seen in a shop back on Station One over Juno. *Very, very expensive but still an admiral's pay-band is up there too,* she thought as she tried to rationalize the purchase.

She continued her mental observation. *Thin but not overly so. Ample in the areas where a woman should be ample and low body fat due to my gym workouts every*

241

other day. Definitely a catch for any man. Too bad I've not met a man who I think is a catch ... always too wrapped up in their careers. She signed.

She smiled as she finished brushing her hair. "Right," she said to herself. "Clean new uniform, and I'll take four Provost guards with me over to the *Crimson I*. Should be enough to make a statement. Being an admiral isn't enough it appears."

She labored through the next few hours on the bridge, finishing reports. She did raise an eyebrow at the latest xeno team report on the recent Issian and Praix tour of the wreck off Ghayth. She noted the one thing she would have gone to first—the technology behind the bridge door security—had as yet not been broached to the Praix. *Would have gone there first to find out how they teleport a missile or projectile aimed at the bridge door thousands of miles into their arctic secure storage. That would be my first real mission. But not the Xeno team,* she thought and sighed.

At her station, there was a small chime, and an icon flashed to let her know she now had only fifteen minutes to get over to the *Crimson I*, which lay nearby. "Not a problem," she said as she closed off a final report and gave the comm to her XO, Lieutenant Commander Nodal Drouhin. He was a career XO. He never wanted to move up, and he never would, which she knew soon after meeting the man on the *Gibraltar* years ago. He was happy being number two, and his attention to detail was amazing—part of the reason she had so much time to herself was his overall love of the ship and all that happened on same.

She smiled at Nodal and said, "Take it easy while I'm off ship, XO."

He shrugged at her, looked down at his console monitor for a split second, and then back at her. "Admiral, I've more than one hundred forty items in my INBOX, so I think I'll be a busy sailor for a while.

There wasn't even a hint of frustration or anger in that answer. In fact, he sounded more like he was proud that he was so busy. *Typical career XO,* she thought, and she smiled back at him as if to commiserate with him. But she knew he'd not want his INBOX any emptier either.

She left the bridge, went down the curved corridor to the lift, and then down to Deck One via the lift. Once she reached Deck One, she headed to the ramp down to the landing port tarmac. Her four Provost guards were there already, and they fell in behind her as she moved down the ramp and over the macadam to the *Crimson I*. A duty officer and a couple of marines met her there. "You're right on time, Ma'am. Please follow me to the meeting room," one of the marines said. It took a few more minutes, but she was eventually sitting in front of Captain Sander, and she smiled.

"Captain, first let me congratulate you on your promotion. You are, I think, the first Issian captain anywhere on the RIM," she said. Her congratulations were sincere. While he had been under her authority in the Barony Navy just a few months back, as he was a friend of Lord Scott— rather Duke d'Avigdor now—he'd been often under his direct command. She'd never really gotten to know Bram, but it looked like that was going to change.

He smiled at her and nodded too. "Admiral, yes, thank you so much for those kind words. I was floored myself when I was asked to captain the *Crimson I*, and I just hope to rise to the occasion. Might I also offer up that I hear very good things about your own abilities from others I know over at the Captains Council as well."

She nodded back. The Captains Council was the group of all Barony Navy captains, which she met with once a month to handle various Barony Navy matters. With now almost thirty ships in the navy and six more on order, including two new Supra destroyers from the Seenra, the Barony Navy was growing.

She looked at him and now raised an eyebrow.

"So, Bram, if I might—what are we doing here in Warlord space?"

He nodded and passed over a hard copy of the full report on what the *Crimson I* had been able to investigate so far. "I'll forward the file to your tablet over on the *Gibraltar* too," Bram said. He then recapped the latest information for her, and he made sure he covered the Noriega situation in depth, including the demands, threats, and everything he assessed as important enough to insure against.

"This Noriega—do you think that if either the Caliphate or the Barony does get Jannah to leave the Warlord space, that he or he and the other warlords might attack the RIM? Or Jannah? Or this Tunander Coalition even?"

He looked away for a moment to seemingly think on that, but then he turned back to face her. "I think that Noriega knows that starting a war with the whole RIM is a suicide mission. But, I do think that if he can find a way to hurt Tunander or Jannah directly, he'd take it in an instant. The warlord is, without a doubt, so full of himself and his power that he thinks no one can do anything but obey his commands. At least that's how I see it, Admiral. He's a warlord to always have a watch on is what I think is good advice here."

She focused on what he said at the closing and

nodded. Good advice indeed, she thought. "And I must ask—who is here on the *Roc* to do the pitch to Jannah?"

Bram knew she asked that because she wanted to know who her competition would be would be. Bram also knew she was more interested in other developments than getting Jannah to join the Barony. Bram looked at her and smiled. "The Roc brought the newest admiral in the Caliphate Navy —Admiral Magnusson. Yes, that Magnusson," he added quickly.

She pursed her lips as though she was going to whistle and leaned back. *The man who had shot one of the Praix and triggered the whole Praix attack back on Ghayth was now an admiral. The man who had supposedly been under the control of the Master Adept at the time. The man who the Master Adept had come to defend at his court martial trial. The same man she had sent to Amasis to a dead-end job on their space station. The man who had resigned his captaincy in the Barony Navy just a few weeks ago had surfaced. He was now an admiral and one that will be fighting me for the Jannah planet.*

She shook her head. "The RIM is one strange small town, is it not, Bram?"

He grinned at her. "Admiral, it is that and more than that. I really think that tomorrow will be an interesting meeting. And I have to update you too

—in the past hour, we received a notice that, at the meeting tomorrow, both other worlds had requested to take a role too—that's Ventos Prime, the huge oil world and Parauda, the military one. Both want seats at the table, and they were granted that right by the Tunander himself, it appears. So add them to the list. You. Me. Magnusson. The Tunander. The Jannah team. Should be one heck of a good time."

She laughed right out loud. "It will be that and then some, Bram. Now can we talk about the price that the Barony—or the Caliphate—might have to pay to get Jannah?" she asked.

Their meeting went on for more than an hour more, and eventually, they had some consensus on items about the upcoming meeting.

She walked back to the *Gibraltar* slowly, enjoying the sunshine and the click of her boots on the macadam too. *Tomorrow will be interesting to say the least ...*

Once again, the team from the *Crimson I* was taking a ride to the Tunander's palace. Just like a few weeks ago, a personnel carrier with a built-in turret and the machine gun guard who watched the street ahead had waited for them.

Bram wondered if he'd ever fired at anyone, but

then he realized this was all show. *Show of strength to the local citizens maybe,* he thought. As they went down the big main street in Crisus, he once again saw the newer buildings. The sidewalk cafés, office towers, and restaurants looked pretty deserted today as the planet-wide holidays were now over.

Ahead they passed through an arched driveway in a solid wide and long building. The stone used to build the structure was a shade of gray with a bit of rusty red mixed in with it. The four vehicles went through that portal which was about thirty feet wide. Inside the archway, there was a courtyard, which must have been a hundred yards square. The building had three stories and a multitude of windows looking down at the wide cobblestone courtyard. The carrier with the guards and the turret gunner pulled off to one side, but their driver instead drove straight across the cobblestones and stopped at what looked like a reception committee.

The vehicle holding Bram and the team from the *Crimson I* was the first to stop and empty. Bram, his XO, Ambassador Harmon, and Major Stal got off and stood waiting for the others. The next carrier held Admiral Magnusson and his XO, a tall Caliphate citizen whom Bram had only met once. Magnusson's XO looked so hawkish that Bram wondered if the alien ate raw flesh. Last today was the vehicle that carried Admiral Vennamo, and she had brought her XO, the Conclusion alien, Drouhin.

The communications officer Sithe Ogrunder greeted them, and everyone walked up the big stairs in front of the huge arched building that was the Tunander's palace. Once inside, Sithe Ogrunder swept them all in and down the hallway, but this time to the right. At the second doorway on the left, he went right through the four guards posted there and into the room. It had been set up the same way Bram would have done it too.

There was a large four-sided table in the center of the room, and each side had many chairs for the attendees. On the table in front of each chair was a pad of paper with stylos, a glass, and a pitcher of ice water. On one wall, the perennial catering table held drinks and the like, and on the other side of the room were a couple of large portable view-screens set up right now to show the planet from low orbit. *The blues and greens and clouds looked so serene and gentle,* Bram thought.

The Tunander was already seated on one side of the four-sided table. Again, he wore an outfit with many colors, badges, medals, and chest ribbons. *The man was a living bulletin board of color,* Bram thought. On his right sat the Jannah agricultural ministry trio with their hands crossed on the desk in front of them. On the warlord's left side sat who Bram believed were the representatives from the other two planets of the Tunander Coalition—Ventos Prime and Parauda.

"Your seats are here," Ogrunder said, and he pointed at the side of the table facing the warlord.

Bram and his group sat, while the twosome from the Caliphate Navy was seated on the side to Bram's left and Admiral Vennamo on his right. *Each of the groups has a side, and each seems balanced, good planning,* he thought. Behind him, he heard the doors close to the room.

The Tunander got started immediately. "Thank you all for your patience on this—we know that this is of great importance, but you must remember that our planetary holidays are also an important part of the Tunander Coalition too. So thank you. We are here today, I understand, to discuss a proposed change in our coalition. A change that, at least at this point, I am not in favor of at all. I believe Captain Sander will address this point now," he said.

His voice, Bram thought, was open and not loaded with any kind of animus, but he had said right out loud that he was against these talks about changes to the coalition.

"Thank you, Tunander. What we find ourselves in is perhaps an exercise in one of the basics of society, the proposed change to how a planet and a group of planets are governed."

It had taken the ambassador more than a few hours to hammer away at this with him all last evening to show that these changes were going to happen anyways. He had worked on this short speech this morning too, and he had it down cold.

"We find that, as a diplomatic mission to the coalition, we were sent here to open up new trade deals with your four planets—and that we will continue to work on. But something else happened. There was an outreach by the Jannah planet," he said as he gestured toward the agricultural team sitting opposite him, "to change their realm. From one within the Tunander Coalition to one within the RIM Confederacy. This is the reason for today's meeting, and I hope that we can look at this and see if there is not something that can be done to effectively aid Jannah in their quest, Tunander."

He stopped then. He didn't look around but kept his stare on the warlord who just stared back.

"A fair way to explain how things are, Captain. Might I now ask the Jannah group—does this represent your own reason for these talks?"

The ambassador had forewarned him last night that this was the exact spot that the talks were focused on—what would the Jannah team say in public in front of their Warlord.

The head of that agricultural team spoke up

slowly and distinctly.

"We, the people of Jannah, yes, are interested in changing our allegiance—from the Tunander Coalition to join the RIM Confederacy. We understand that there are two avenues to do that— either we join as a sub-realm under a full Confederacy membership or as a full member ourselves. We have chosen to join as a sub-realm, and that is why the Caliphate and the Barony are here today to present their offers. We would also make it a point that the coalition be compensated for this change—but in a reasonable fashion too."

Bingo, Bram thought. *They'd taken the full bite on the apple and had made the comment that the Tunander be compensated too for their departure from the Coalition.*

For a moment, they all sat and contemplated what the Jannah representative said and then the Tunander spoke once more.

"Before we get to those presentations, I am supposed to ask if either the Ventos Prime or Parauda planets have any comment to make at this time?"

The leaders from both planets looked at each other, and then the Ventos Prime planet leader spoke up.

"We—Ventos Prime and Parauda—are simply here to watch and listen and learn. We have both agreed to say that we are not interested in leaving the Tunander Coalition at this time—subject to change, of course. So at this point, we will just wait and see."

Interesting, Bram thought. *They want to be here to see what the presentations are going to be and to figure out if a good deal can be struck.* He shook his head slightly, thinking this was a great strategy, when from behind him, the closed doors to the room banged open.

The whole room reacted by turning to look at the doorway, and they were shocked to see the four guards posted there to protect the room lay in a pile outside the doorway. Striding into the room, Warlord Noriega held his head high as more than twenty of his own marines, stunners drawn, followed him. The marines took up positions around the room to hold the meeting attendees prisoners, and Noriega smiled at them all.

"As I was told about this meeting, I said no, couldn't happen without me. I didn't get my invitation, Tunander, and I wonder why that might be. In any case, I see that this is the meeting about the future of the coalition—and I have that already figured out for you all," he said.

Bram, the ambassador, his XO, and Alver had dipped a hand down their laps, turning on the power belts to make them all invulnerable.

"Especially to stunners," Bram said to himself. "Especially to bullies who crash meetings," he added to himself.

Tunander almost choked on his shouted answer. "YOU have no right to be here—you are on my own planet, and that gives you no rights at all. And the reason for this meeting is something—once again—you have no right to know."

He rose in his seat, and Noriega gave a short gesture to the marine closest to him, who thumbed his stunner and blasted the rising warlord right down into his seat.

"That was the lowest setting, Tunander—so while movement is now beyond your abilities, you can hear and see what I have to say," he said as he slid a hip over the edge of the table and looked around at the whole group.

"I am Noriega. My own group has six planets, and I would like to add more. Perhaps what I might do is to simply take this coalition and make it a part of my own group. I have not decided upon that, but know this and know this well. I do not take lightly the intrusion of the RIM Confederacy within Warlord space. You, and all like you, are now banned from all of Warlord space—what you used to call Pentyaan space. Get out. Stay out. I have the full weight of almost twenty worlds behind me as both other warlords have agreed to my terms."

He slid off the table and stood up to face Bram
directly, his hands on his hips. "You will leave in
three days. Or we will launch a war upon the
Tunander Coalition to destroy you. And that
includes also your little digging operations over on
R17 as well—we've no idea what you've found, but
leave it too. No more RIM Confederacy ships in
Warlord space. You have been warned. The next
warnings will carry nukes."

Bram sighed. *Would love to tell—or show—this little
tin horn dictator that the Crimson I is invulnerable and
I can't be hurt with stunners, but surprise is always
best.* Bram shook his head. *Better he not know—
should violence occur, these invulnerabilities would be so
much more surprising.*

Bram waved his hand at Alver, who was starting
to get up, to keep him away from Noriega. "We
have heard you, Noriega. We do not like what it is
you've said—and we will discuss this with
Tunander. And you will be notified about our
decision on whether or not to comply. Oh and
wherever this R17 place is, it's free space—which
means that anyone can visit anytime—at least for
the rest of the galaxy, that's what that term means."

The warlord shrugged. "We need no notification.
If your ships are in Warlord space—anywhere in
Warlord space—in three days from today, then our

answer is simple. War." He turned on his heel and spun. Guarded by his marines, he went out the door, and they were gone.

The meeting was broken up quickly after that. "The meeting is adjourned for today," Tunander declared, "and we will reconvene tomorrow. At that time, I will have a position on what the coalition should do."

There were no goodbyes and everyone streamed out around the palace guards who'd been stunned at max and would be unconscious for hours still.

Riding back in the vehicles, there was no talk at all, but Bram did use his PDA to ask if both admirals would come over to the *Crimson I* this evening for a dinner meeting. *There is much to discuss ... including war ...*

CHAPTER NINE

Yesterday's meeting, having been broken up by Warlord Noriega, had reconvened this morning. *Same palace, same room, same table, and same attendees ... hope today's outcome is better,* Bram thought.

Bram sat and listened as the Barony representatives made a presentation with the offer from the Baroness. Once finished, the Caliphate team presented the Caliph's offer. *Both offers are similar so far,* Bram thought. *Both make the standard RIM Confederacy sub-realm offer, and both offer to complete this in a quick manner.*

"Before I finalize my presentation, there is something else I wish to add," Admiral Magnusson said. "There is a current shortfall between the Caliphate and Hope, the planet the Jannah team is so interested in. Hope owes millions of credits to the Caliphate, and the Caliph could provide these solar-powered desalination devices—and the patents perhaps as well—as a bonus." Magnusson paused and looked directly at the Jannah agricultural minister. "The costs for those items would be zero, and that would be a part of the offer itself."

That got some raised eyebrows around the table. Ambassador Harmon nudged Bram and said, "Nice one."

Now it is a done deal, Bram thought, and sure enough, when the Jannah agricultural minister asked to speak, he announced that they would take the Caliphate offer. *No surprise there,* Bram thought. *The Jannah team was swayed by that last item the Caliphate offered.*

Tunander nodded and said, "Then I take it we've come to a decision." Everyone at the table nodded, and the warlord continued.

"So with the offer being made to and then accepted by the Jannah government, we are halfway done with the business of today. The only thing left is to have the Caliphate now tell me, the Warlord of the Tunander Coalition, what they will be giving up to us for this deal to actually happen. Admiral?" he said.

"Now the real dealing begins", Bram said to himself and he leaned back in his chair.

Admiral Magnusson smiled at the warlord. "The Caliphate has not given me any authority to offer anything—even one thin credit—to the Tunander Coalition. The Jannah world has decided to leave the coalition. End of story."

Ambassador Harmon slid a hand down to his lap, and Bram thought about turning on his power belt also, but he decided not to.

The warlord just stared at the admiral. His eyes were wide, and there was a look of both surprise and frustration on his face at the same time.

The room was silent.

Bram sat as well and stared, like everyone was, at the warlord. *This was, perhaps, the crux of the whole matter.*

"I am an economist, which—I would be the first one to admit—is not a background for a warlord. I should have had more experience in war and the military and the violence of using force to get one's way. But instead, I happened to be an economist, and that means that I understand, well, the economy.

"So the Tunander Coalition is going to lose one-fourth of our base—Jannah is a revenue-producing planet. And now they are leaving. One part of me wants to just declare war on the Caliphate. One part of me realizes that this is not the way to go.

"So here's what I propose. Jannah can do as they

please. And the coalition will negotiate directly with the Caliph—if he will speak to us on that basis. This is my decision," he said.

Bram had no idea if that was good or bad for the Caliphate, but there would be no force by Tunander to try to keep his coalition together here in Warlord space.

"But one more thing," the warlord said. "I need to ask—even though as Captain Sander noted, R17 is out in free space—what might the RIM be doing there? It's an empty system—no sentients on either planet, a couple of huge gas giants, and not much else."

Bram answered quickly in the hopes that Admiral Vennamo would keep quiet. "I have no idea, but I will Ansible back to see what Noriega meant—most likely it's just him spouting off with nothing behind that accusation. But, I must ask, Tunander—what will need to be done by us all to circumvent the threats by Noriega?"

Warlord Tunander shrugged. "War is not good for anyone's economy—so I'm against it, of course. But," he said as he looked down the table at the delegation from Parauda, "we do have a realm that does one thing and one thing well—Parauda."

The colonel who sat in the meeting nodded and spoke. "We understand threats—and we know how to deal with them. If called upon to defend the coalition, we will respond with our own usual response—military action."

That got nods from the Ventos Prime members, and the meeting once again broke up.

On the way back to the landing port, Ambassador Harmon leaned over to talk with Bram. "Are we heading back? That three-day deadline from Noriega is now down one day."

"We are not. The *Roc* and the *Gibraltar* are leaving later today, but the *Crimson I* will stay put. I think that should Noriega want to test us—the *Crimson I* is more than up to that," Bram said and smiled.

Later after fielding an EYES ONLY from Admiral Vennamo and letting her in on what R17 was—Birdland and the asteroid mine for Xithricite —they said their goodbyes. She did add that she intended to visit Birdland and look over the mining operation itself.

Late that night, Bram sat in his quarters and wondered what Gia might be up to and how he could get his name on her visitors list. He wanted to see her once again. Bram sighed. *I want to take her out for a date ... a dinner or a concert or a video ... anything to be near her, but that will probably be some time away ...*

#####

Magnusson sat and preened himself as the EYES ONLY Ansible went through and the screen in his Ready room on the Roc faded to black. Moments later, the face of his Caliph came on screen and he smiled at his admiral.

"So, admiral, do I take the smile on your face to be good news?"

Magnusson smiled even more.

"Your grace—yes, I was able to secure the Jannah planet as our newest sub-realm, Caliph. There are some items which I know will not be a problem for us, but that you should know too. May I explain, Caliph?"

"Please, admiral…I'm sure that they are minor details."

Magnusson went on to explain how he'd claimed that there was a trade shortfall between the Caliphate and Hope, and how he'd sweetened the Caliphate offer by offering that the distillation equipment and patents too, were going to be given to Jannah. He had also agreed that there would be some talks between the Caliphate and Tunander too, on what kind of compensation might be a fair trade for Jannah.

The Caliph stared at him, his face a mask.

He had sent a brand new admiral to make a deal for a new realm.

He got the new realm.

Now he had to deal with the deal itself.

So he looked back at his admiral and smiled. Bigger than last time too.

"My choice for admiral is paying dividends already," the Caliph said.

"The Hope trade shortfall is an easy one for me to use to get the Jannah what they want—so good call. The price however we might pay the Coalition for that planet is another story. Maybe I'll up the ante and see how we can buy all three of the other planets too."

Magnusson then went into a fully drilled down report on the whole meeting—the first day and then the meeting the second day too. He also let the Caliph know, that threats from Noriega were made and that either the Roc had to be out of the Warlord space—or face nukes. At least that's what the Warlord said.

The Caliph took it all in, and from what Magnusson could see, he even made some notes too.

He spoke though as he'd made his decision.

"You said that the *Crimson I* will be staying on. It will therefore be that ship—clad in Xithricite, that Noriega will try to attack and that means that he and his ships will be destroyed. So, with the Gibraltar leaving today—you will return back to Neria today as well. I still will have a say with the

Crimson I and it's captain as the Caliphate is still a full partner on that mission. So, come home, admiral—have your dinner tonight with me here in the Palace tents. I look forward to dining with you this evening, admiral."

Magnusson smiled once more and the EYES ONLY screen faded to black...

#####

As the *Gibraltar* jumped back into real space around R17, the helmsman said, "Admiral this is her—R17. No sentient life the AI reports, and Gallipedia agrees with that audit, Ma'am."

They had left the Tunander Coalition just a few minutes ago and had jumped to R17 and found the planet.

"Plain, big oceans and landmasses. No sentients ... too bad too, because the place looks wonderful," her XO said as he worked on his console. On the view-screen, there were sweeping views of beaches and mountains and even of an oasis on the desert somewhere too. *He was impressed,* Eleanor thought. *At least one of us is because for me, a good planet with no sentient life is a waste.*

The *Gibraltar* was in high orbit around the planet, and from there, they could easily see the asteroid ring around the planet and the moon, which hung in the same ring of asteroids. The asteroids ranged in size from what looked like miles across to yards, and somewhere in there was the asteroid with the Xithricite mine. The XO provided her with that asteroid's coordinates.

"Helmsman, Outside the plane of the ring of the asteroid belt, then take us in when she's close," she ordered.

The helmsman was good. He took the ship up and off the plane of the ring, and then the *Gibraltar* turned to port. Using InertialDrive, it went along, the view-screen showing the now red-bordered asteroid still ahead. It took ten minutes, but the *Gibraltar* eventually hung right above the red asteroid on the screen, and the helmsman yawed the ship to the right and then down toward the asteroid. In two more minutes, the ship hung above an asteroid, as the helmsman slowed the ship and then had her stop with her side right up to the *Callisto*, which was on the planet side of the asteroid.

"Ansible—let the *Callisto* know that we're going to send down a shuttle to the asteroid. I want to see it right up close," she said and gave the comm to her XO.

She took the lift down to the shuttle deck and was met by two Provost guards, who were going to accompany her. "Always a step ahead and looking out for my safety. Drouhin's a good XO," she said to herself. Twenty minutes later, the shuttle set down on the asteroid and placed itself on the floor of the crater that lay ahead.

She struggled to get into her spacesuit, and then with the two guards, she air-locked out to the surface and looked around. Off to the side, the crater went for hundreds of yards. Ahead, there was another shuttle with wide-p[en cargo bays and what looked like some sheets of the ore already on board. She climbed the edge of the crater and went over the top to look at the mine area itself. Against an outcrop of the red ore from the tail end of the meteorite, the miners had erected three scaffoldings around the thirty-foot-wide ore block. One of the crew stood up top, and around his waist, he had tied and supported the metal framework of the saw. Below him and off to either side, two more crew were standing, and their jobs were to swing the saw from side to side from the focal point above, held by the man on top.

It looked like very slow work, but once the sheet was free, the pieces were all carted off by other crew and stored in the shuttle for transport back to the Callisto later on. She talked to the miners on their comm channel, and they commiserated on hard work in general.

As she was watching the actual mining, a shadow went over her and the whole asteroid. She backed up, turned to look up at the planet, and froze.

Above her was a ship—a destroyer like the *Gibraltar*—but the icon logo she could see said it belonged to the Warlord Noriega. It had come from the dark side of the asteroid, moving now slowly along the planet side as it cut out the light from same. It was sneaking up on the *Gibraltar*, using the asteroid itself to hide it's ambush of the two Barony ships on the other side.

"Shit," she said, and following her first instinct, she radioed to all the miners to take cover. Then she realized that was impossible on the small asteroid— a destroyer could simply drop a nuke on it, and they'd all go up in vapor.

"The shuttle ... get to my shuttle," she said, and she turned to head back as a huge flash of light struck her. She was slow getting the helmet visor to filter down the view, and all she could see was the brilliant yellow light across each eye. She had to stop running as she couldn't see at all. She radioed to all to hold their ground until they could see better.

It took more than ten minutes for her to be able to see, and in that time, she counted nine more huge flashes but these flashes weren't as bright as that first one. A guard had grabbed her by the arm, and she was hustled into the shuttle. The guard told the pilot to get her up and back to the *Gibraltar*.

While her vision was still filled with strobe-like

267

streaks across her pupils, she still saw the pilot turn to face her, his face white.

"Can't, Ma'am, the attacker took out the *Gibraltar* with six nukes, and she fell into the planet, Ma'am."

She was in shock. She'd just lost her ship and more than six hundred crew and officers.

She was in a shuttle on an asteroid, and the enemy was above her.

"The *Callisto* then? Is she there?"

"Ma'am, they jumped after the second nuke hit the *Gibraltar*. Dunno where they went—but we're alone, Ma'am. And the enemy ship is doing a turnaround to come back. We'll be in range in less than a minute." There was strain in his voice strain that she'd heard before.

"Then take us down, right into the atmosphere of Birdland—at InertialDrive max. AI—admiral code U-eight-eight-six. Get us the hell outta here, and evasive action all the way down. Get us safe, Lieutenant! And send out an all channels, Ansible, that we're under attack …" she barked at him. The admiral code would get AI to release the throttle governors and allow the pilot to make the best speed that the shuttle could. And if possible, the RIM would be notified that they needed help.

The shuttle lifted up, yawed to the left, and then jumped to full max speed, shooting toward the planet.

"Put the enemy on screen—left half," she ordered, and in seconds, she could see the enemy destroyer, turning still about ten thousand miles away over the asteroid field.

"Put the estimates for intersect of our flight path on the sidebar," she ordered.

On the sidebar, a quick line drawing quickly appeared and showed the face of the planet the shuttle was running to for safety and the slowly turning enemy destroyer well off to one side. The estimate of how long it would take until their flight paths intersected appeared. "Two minutes and fourteen seconds until intersect," the admiral said, and that time stamp went down another second.

We have two minutes and a bit to run and to hide ... if we can, that is, she thought ...

CHAPTER TEN

"Sir, I've got an Ansible SOS from the *Gibraltar* —well, from a shuttle of theirs, Captain."

The bridge Ansible officer had already hit the button for the klaxons, and they were beginning to blare all over the ship.

"What the hell? On screen now," Bram said, and he hit the CODE RED button on his captain's chair console, and BATTLE STATIONS appeared on all screens throughout the ship.

On the bridge view-screen, the interior of a shuttle with some people he didn't recognize appeared, and then Admiral Vennamo stood up leaning on the back of the seat in front of her.

"Anyone—this is Admiral Vennamo of the *Gibraltar*. I'm told that she took six hits—nukes— from a Noriega destroyer not more than twenty minutes ago. I was off ship on the Xithricite mining asteroid over Birdland—sorry, off R17 as it's known here in Warlord space. We're fleeing the enemy destroyer, going down to the planet, and we'll try to find somewhere to hide. SOS code seven-seven-Y," she said, and then the message repeated itself over and over.

"Kill that," Bram said, and then he looked at his helmsman. "Get us the hell over to Birdland now, Helm. I want it to be in less than a minute—no landing authority or requests—just go now!" he yelled.

In twenty seconds, the *Crimson I* lifted off going to full InertialDrive when they were less than five hundred feet up, and in ten seconds more, they went to sub-space as the Barony Drive kicked in. Ten seconds later, they popped into real-time space over Birdland, and the mass detector sirens went off. Not more than a half mile away was a destroyer —an enemy destroyer from Noriega.

He barked at the Ansible officer and said, "Get that captain on the horn, NOW!"

Moments later, the view-screen showed a face, and it was the face of Noriega himself.

"You are in Warlord space. Like the ship I just took down a few minutes ago, one that you'd have to agree makes your little frigate look like a toy, I give you a choice. Leave or die," he said, and the

271

screen went black again.

Bram looked over to Major Stal and said, "Major, get a team ready to go out on the *Defiant* and get our shuttle people. Full rescue and recovery, please."

The major left the bridge in a hurry.

"Helm, find me the *Gibraltar* below. I want longitudes and latitudes for same, and get those coordinates to Alver on the *Defiant* too.

He turned to his XO. "XO, I want a spread of torpedoes—full strength nukes, please, at contact detonations, engine, and life support targets. Ready to launch on my command. Helm, take me in closer to their ship—say, five hundred yards off. Ansible, send them a simple order—leave or die." He smiled and waited.

In a minute, the sidebar up on the view-screen chimed as those items were all ticked off. As he'd hoped, the destroyer had swung to its starboard side about thirty degrees to bring a full battery of its own weapons to bear.

"Engage the enemy," Bram said, his voice strong.

From the side, he could see the missiles carrying the nukes head out those short yards to the destroyer. The destroyer's laser radar had picked up same, and they were able to knock out four of them, but the other two hit the destroyer full, in the rear engine areas. While the blast and the detonations were massive, in space, they were not heard or felt. The view-screen showed the flash of light that the atomic explosions had generated.

And from the side of the destroyer, from their huge amidships arrays, out came a full dozen missiles, nukes once again, and all aimed at the heart of the *Crimson I*. The missiles crossed the last few hundred yards, and they hit the red metal Xithricite plates of the *Crimson I*'s hull, and nothing happened.

No explosions. No piercing of the plates. No nukes. Nothing.

"Engage," Bram said once more as the *Defiant* was launched down toward Birdland to find the shuttle.

The six nukes roared away from the *Crimson I* toward the destroyer, and this time, the targets were life support systems and all three landing bays. The landing bays exploded killing all close inside the destroyer.

"Target their weapons arrays next, XO," Bram shouted as this time the destroyer was aiming their plasma cannons at them.

The cannons fired and two balls of gaseous plasma roared across the space aimed directly at the *Crimson I*'s bridge. Both hit the red metal hull plating, and both were snuffed out completely.

The balls of plasma, at more than ten thousand

degrees, did not burn through the metal. They went out like a snuffed candle.

"Should be getting the idea soon. Engage," Bram said, and from the *Crimson I*, out went another six nukes, their last bank of atomics.

This time, the missiles were aimed at the weapons arrays amidships and the plasma cannons at the bow and rear of the destroyer. A laser did catch one, but the rest found their targets. The destroyer lay badly hurt and injured.

"She's done, Captain," Daika said, but her hands were still poised over her console ready to keep going.

"Sir," the helmsman yelled, "She's firing up her —"

The destroyer blinked out of real-time space as she jumped to FTL using her TachyonDrive.

"Helm, get us down over the wreck of the *Gibraltar* if you can get any idea of the coordinates from Major Stal," Bram said as he killed the klaxons and stood his crew down off BATTLE STATIONS.

Admiral Vennamo had been found on the shuttle with the rest of the miners and her guards just a few hundred yards from the wreck of the *Gibraltar*. It had taken four hours, but all were now on the *Crimson I*.

For the *Gibraltar* and its crew, there was no hope. She'd been nuked up in space, losing her hull structure and life support at the same time. She had arrowed in, driving a crater almost a mile wide on a high steppe near the mountains on a southern continent. Thankfully, the steppe was grass and weed and overgrowth bound; had it been a forest, the fires would have burned for a month. As it was, the ship's safety AI had taken over, and as she had plowed into the ground, everything had been turned off or ejected to drift down on its own. There had been no resulting fires and no further damage to the archives and systems that had been turned off and then shielded with the security force fields.

Still, Bram thought as he read the first reports. *More than six hundred and thirty dead.*

There was no way to be exact yet since a team would need to come from Neres City to provide full post-mortem on the ship and its crew.

After being released from sickbay, Admiral Vennamo had stormed onto the bridge. She wanted blood — Noriega's blood. "I want you — us, I mean, to go to Noriega and arrest the warlord. I understand that you've both received the *Callisto's* report and you've seen it too. Shows the Noriega destroyer coming up and around the mining asteroid and launching nukes. No warning. No notice. A pure ambush and they chose the *Gibraltar*, as she was a destroyer, just hanging in space—not with BATTLE STATIONS on the ready or shields up. No warning. And I want that man's blood," she yelled right on the bridge.

Bram nodded. He was the captain of the *Crimson I*, and even though she was an admiral, he had no real reason to follow her orders—except that he wanted to.

He called for a quick meeting, and soon the admiral, his XO, the major, and the ambassador sat in his ready room.

He went right to Alver first and asked, "If we land, can you and your marines find this Noriega and arrest him and get him back to the *Crimson I*?"

"Roger that, and we can do it quickly. I cannot guarantee no casualties on their part—they will fight back. But with belts on, we will be an unstoppable force."

Bram nodded and then turned to the XO. "And can you handle the *Crimson I* on the deck? If we land, the ship is just as protected as always, but the landing ramps can't be used as that opens up the Xithricite hull plating, right?"

The XO replied, "No problem, Sir, but aren't you going to be on the bridge?"

"That's a negative. I'm going with the marines to

grab this warlord. Wouldn't miss it!" Bram said as he looked at the ambassador. "And Ambassador — exactly how many laws are we breaking if we do this?"

Ambassador Harmon smiled. "Well, I believe the phrase we might want to use is 'hot pursuit.' We are in hot pursuit of the criminal who shot down one of the RIM Confederacy member realm's ships. So we can pursue and then arrest the perp — perpetrator I mean by that — and that's law just about everywhere!"

Bram grinned. "Admiral, it will be a real privilege to have you on my bridge" — she rose to make a point, but he stopped her — "And yes, I know, you're coming along too. Noted. And now, let's go get this warlord," he said.

#####

The trip from Birdland to Noriega took only seconds using the Barony Drive, and as soon as they arrived and popped back into real space, the klaxons went off. Surrounding the area in low orbit above the planet were three destroyers and a handful of cruisers. All had shields up, and all bristled with weapons arrays at the ready.

"XO, I want scans down below on the capital city — we want the warlord's location. Ansible, talk to whomever thinks they're in charge up here. Tell them we want Warlord Noriega for the unprovoked attack and destruction of a RIM Confederacy ship, the *Gibraltar*."

He sat in the captain's chair, and like the rest of the bridge crew, he waited for a reply or sign of action. On one side of him sat Admiral Vennamo and the Ambassador, both staring at the view-screen sidebar. Major Stal stood off to his left and was already wearing full marine armor, and he carried his helmet under his arm. Everyone on the ship was ready, and the message of BATTLE STATIONS was displayed everywhere. The red light from the alert cast an eerie glow all over the bridge.

The wait was not long, and the view-screen now changed from an orbital shot of the planet below to a man's face.

"Admiral Ginert here. You are intruding on the Noriega space—you are required to leave in one minute, else face the combined firepower of all the vessels you see here."

He looked like he was serious, and Bram couldn't resist. "Admiral—I am sure that by now you've heard about the unprovoked attack on a RIM Confederacy vessel—the *Gibraltar*—by one of your own Noriega Navy ships. The *Gibraltar* was destroyed—along with more than six hundred crewmen and officers. We also fought off the

278

attacking ship, which is probably trying to limp home, but at TachyonDrive speeds, it will be a while.

"You should, however, read any reports that they've sent back to you on our ship—pay careful attention to the parts that state it is invulnerable to your attacks of any kind of weapon.

"We also know that this attack was threatened by your warlord himself. So we are here to arrest your dictator and take him back to the RIM Confederacy for trial. You will turn over the warlord to us, now."

His voice had been firm but polite. He had spelled out for the admiral what was expected. He had not specified a time frame to adhere to though, he realized, so he added that now. "And you now have five minutes to turn over your warlord for trial. Else, we will do that ourselves."

There, Bram thought, *that spells it out even easier for him.*

The view-screen went dark as the admiral cut his connection off and they waited. On the view-screen sidebar, a set of coordinates appeared for Warlord Noriega with the notation that AI had located the warlord and placed him in the administration building below on the planet's landing port. Second floor of that building was as close as the AI could place him, but that was good enough for RIM marines.

When the first minute of the five Bram had given Admiral Ginert passed, Bram expected the *Crimson I* would be taking hits—but that did not happen.

As the deadline of five minutes that he had set came closer, Bram rose. "XO, the comm is yours, unless the admiral would rather ..."

Vennamo waved him off.

"We're on our way, track the Defiant, and let us know about any updates," Bram saved and he followed Alver to the lift, down to the shuttle deck, and aboard the *Defiant*.

Along for the ride were twenty more marines, all suited, armed, and, of course, wearing their power belts. Bram clicked his belt on and smiled at Alver. Bram too had donned the same suit as the marines, and at his side, the weapon of choice for this kind of work when wearing a power belt, was his .454 Casull revolver.

"Let's get this done, Major," he said, and the *Defiant* swung out of the *Crimson I* shuttle bay and twisted as she dove to the planet's surface.

Three of the Noriega ships lying there launched a few quick missiles at the *Defiant*. And hit they did, but as the *Defiant* was clad in the red metal Xithricite hull plating, all three of the missiles were snuffed out. No explosions. No penetration of the *Defiant*'s hull either. It was no surprise to the XO who watched from above and no surprise to Bram on board the *Defiant* either.

"That might show them that we're here to do what we said," he said, and those in the landing bay nodded.

They flew down at Mach 3, and then the pilot swerved at the last moment to halt the ship perfectly above the tarmac on the landing field. There were no other ships down at this moment, which made sense, Bram figured, as they'd all be up above to try to threaten the *Crimson I* with sheer numbers.

Didn't work, he thought and grinned to himself. He nodded to Alver as he got his own helmet. "Your show, Major—let's go!" Like the other marines, Bram got in the lineup as the landing ramp jutted out of the *Defiant* and then banged down on the macadam.

"Building straight ahead, second floor. Rules of engagement—no aggression by us. You may wound if needed, but no casualties if at all possible," played in Bram's helmet speakers as he ran with the squad. They went straight across the tarmac and were met by no one. Well in the distance stood three guards near what looked like an access point into the landing field. They stood and watched but did nothing else.

Good, Bram thought as he pounded along behind the marines.He realized he was slowly falling behind and two marines were flanking him at his own pace. He tried to speed up a bit, and they kept pace too. The entrance to the building came up quickly in front of the running group.

The major went up the stairs and then across a big rotunda that was totally deserted. As they all climbed the stairs, Bram heard from his XO in his helmet.

"Sir, still status quo here. Two of the cruisers, however, have made the jump to FTL —destination unknown at this point, Sir."

Bram said, "Roger," and he turned on the landing to take the final bank of stairs up to the second floor.

The major had stopped there to look at his PDA, and he said, "To starboard."

Everyone heard that on their helmet speakers and followed Major Stal as he strode that way, down a long corridor with many doorways—all closed. Ahead, at the end of the hallway, was a set of big, wide-open double doors. As they drew closer, Bram could see guards stood at attention inside those doors.

Bram's group entered the massive room. There was nothing on the walls but what looked like mirrors that reflected what lay in the room.

Noriega himself sat on what Bram would call a throne. *A throne room in the admin building on the landing port? Odd,* Bram thought. Noriega remained seated, and he stared at them all with no sense of any kind of submission on his face or in his demeanor either.

On that throne at the top sat a big globe of the planet Noriega. It was lit from within and slowly turning on its axis.

Bram slid through the group of marines that were now fanning out. *Must be to spread their firepower,* Bram thought. No sooner than he thought that, the marines all spun to point outward and away from the warlord. They were all now pointed at the fifty guards who were in the room with them but still standing at attention. All were armed with some kind of rifles, and yet not a one was ready to take any kind of aggressive action.

Looking at his major, Bram took off his helmet, tucked it under his arm, and was about to speak when the warlord yelled at him.

"You were warned. You knew what the consequences would be if you stayed in Warlord space. And your destroyer paid for your failure to obey me," he shouted. Noriega was dressed as always with that big display of patches that meant nothing to anyone else, and he leaned forward as he shouted at them.

Bram stepped forward one more step, and as he did, he heard three chimes from the throne room's

AI. The chimes meant nothing to him, but those chimes must have been a signal, as the warlord's men suddenly broke from their attention poses, and each one took a step back with his right foot only. The rifles came up, and the clicks of safeties being disengaged rung around the room.

"You have one minute to leave the room and return to your ship—and then out of our Warlord space." The warlord smiled. "One minute," he shouted once again.

Bram thought he could see the man's spittle as he lifted himself partially from the throne. *What's that line about power being a corruption ...* he thought as he smiled at the warlord.

"Warlord Noriega—we are here to arrest you, as you are charged with the crime of an unprovoked attack upon the *BN Gibraltar* and the murder of more than six hundred crew. You will come with us —now—or we will take you in by force," he said. It was the most satisfying thing he'd ever said as a new captain, and that made him proud.

"YOU have been warned again. Colonel, shoot this man," he said.

From behind Bram, one of the Noriega guards strode up to take a spot just to Bram's left. He raised his rifle, aimed it squarely at Bram's chest, and fired. The sound was loud in the big room.

The bullet must have hit me—yet I feel nothing,

Bram thought. *No penetration, no inertia from the mass and speed of the bullet. Nothing.*

He smiled at the incredulous look on the colonel's face and then looked back at the warlord. "You cannot hurt us—any of us—Warlord. So your choice is to either step down off that throne or face the consequences." He kept smiling as he drew his .454 Casull, pointed it up at the globe above the Warlord's head, and pulled the trigger. The kick of the revolver was big and it jumped back with recoil.

The bursting of the globe above the warlord's head when the bullet hit it was bigger. Liquid spilled out and showered all over Noriega, soaking him.

That also appeared to initialize the throne room AI to attack as well, and while no marine was hurt, there were lasers that tried to pierce their armor for a whole minute. Green lancing rays were sent from behind those mirrors on the walls to try to strike the marines, and while each of them was perfectly accurate, none of them worked. After that minute, they stopped, and a speaker somewhere in the room said, "AI response was accurate. Body count zero."

Bram nodded to the warlord as he gestured to Alver and said, "Take him."

The warlord jumped to his feet, but Alver was quicker. He wrestled the warlord down to the floor, and two marines put him in handcuffs and dragged him to his feet.

"Colonel, what you've just seen is the strength of the RIM Confederacy. We have taken the warlord into custody, and he will go on trial for his crimes. With the charges against him, I would think you'll never see Noriega again, so with that in mind, I ask that you—and whatever will now pass as the government of this planet—rethink upon your next leader.

"I have been told that if you wish to come to the RIM and speak to our own government for help, that can be accommodated to. We will leave now, go up to the *Crimson I,* and then back to RIM Confederacy space. But we will be back as Jannah is now a sub-realm member of the RIM Confederacy.

"Good luck, Colonel … you just may need it, Sir," Bram said as he spun to leave the room to go back up to the *Crimson I.*

#####

Bram thanked the Duke for his third time on tonight's EYES ONLY Ansible call and smiled as the screen went dark.

It appeared that on his first ever mission as a duchy

captain, he'd done well.

Well, at least the Duke thought so.

He had, with great help from the Ambassador, gotten the planet Jannah to join the RIM Confederacy under the Caliphate realm.

That was a good thing, Tanner had said.

He had also, with what the Ambassador had called 'inadvertent diplomacy,' gotten the Warlord Tunander to consider dealing with the Caliph on some kind of repayment plan—one that admiral Magnusson had already intimated meant joining the Caliphate itself if that could be managed.

Another good thing, the duke had said.

Without it being Bram's fault, the Gibraltar had been lost, but he had helped get the admiral out of trouble. And that had led to his crippling of the Noriega ship that had destroyed the Gibraltar sending her packing.

Another good thing and that too got him a ducal thanks.

And lastly his assault with the major on the Warlord's planet and the arrest of Noriega himself. Taken into custody, the man was below in the Crimson I brig waiting to get to the Barony where he would be held till his trial. He heard that the admiral, Vennamo went down every so often, just to look at the man who was still ranting and raving it seemed on the inadmissability of any kind of evidence against him and that he was not subject to their authority to hold him and try him for any crimes. He was a Warlord—he made the laws and had to obey none of them.

The duke had very much enjoyed the story of the throne room incident and again, Bram had gotten thanks.

And lastly, here on Tunander, where the Crimson I had stopped by, he had just had an audience with the Warlord and had let him know that should the Caliphate not offer him what he thought was a good recompense for his losing Jannah, that perhaps other RIM Confederacy realms might do just that...

He nodded to his helmsman to take them home and the duchy sun slowly centered itself in the bridge view-screen...and they jumped to FTL...

Epilogue ~

Tanner watched Gia slide her foot across her thigh and rub at a spot on her instep. He wondered if he should do anything more for her. She had no idea that as he was the duke, he could make allowances in her house arrest details.

He thought he would enlarge her visitors list. There had been two requests already from someone at Gallipedia to have an interview with her for the galaxy database.

He had no real clue if an interview was an idea he wanted to authorize, he thought, and he tucked a foot under his thigh and sat back in the big chair in his private study to watch his sister as she watched a movie in her living room.

Gallipedia visitor and an interview might be a good thing, and then again, depending on what the article said about Gia, it might be a bad one, Tanner thought as he rubbed his temples.

He already knew, as Helena had looked it up and printed it off to stick under his nose just a month ago, that the new Duke d'Avigdor had some interesting history. He tried not to think of it, but he was pleased when he saw there had been mention and emphasis on the fact that he had been found not guilty of any kind of negligence in the death of his sister Nora those long years ago.

He watched as Gia twisted to reach into a bowl of green grapes on the little table at the side of the couch and tossed a couple into her mouth. She always had liked grapes. He remembered when they were growing up on Branton, they used to play with them, and she would throw one that he'd try to catch in his mouth. *Brother and sister fun.* He laughed as that memory played back.

After watching Gia for a few more minutes, he killed the feed to her apartment.

Getting up, he went to the big doors that opened up onto the balcony on the third floor of the palace and went out to stand against the railing. He looked up and noted that at this time of year, nighttime on Neen meant that the skies were pointed out of the Milky Way galaxy and toward the blackness beyond. He could, if he squinted just right, see peripherally the SagD galaxy and, yes, Andromeda too. But the rest was just deep, deep blackness.

He remembered a professor of astrophysics in a class at the Kinross Navy had spoken about that blackness. According to science, he had stated, the blackness would slowly give way to distant galaxies as time went on. He said that in a billion years, that blackness would be so full of new light from galaxies that it would be hard to even see a dark spot.

Tanner hadn't known what to think about that. If

that was true, then the light was already on its way. *Just have to wait for it to get here.. Or the prof was full of it, and the deep, deep blackness would never be lit up.*

Either way, it made no sense for him to worry about it. After all, a billion years was a long, long time.

BOOK FOURTEEN OF THE RIM CONFEDERACY

Prison Break

Prologue ~

Helena sat, thinking *it still needs something.*

Or some things, maybe to make the Aviary a really good place to sit and meditate—at least for me.

She had ordered many items that so far, had worked she thought, as she sat in the corner of a large divan, her feet tucked up and nestled below her. The divan faced the fine fencing of the large avian space and she'd had it placed about in the middle. Some of the plants that had been in a viewers way, she'd had her aides remove them and one could see now from the divan and the whole rest of the seating group, just about all the space inside.

She noted too, that the birds had adapted to the changes within their space by simply ignoring them.

Birds were like that, she'd read. In fact over the past month, she'd been haunting the Galipedia areas that covered aviary ownership and the handling of birds of all types. She did note that the couple of species in her Aviary, that looked so oddly, were not given any kind of a Galipedia entry —that was something she thought that she would do herself but later.

Once the Aviary was finished, she thought, *that would be the right time to do that.*

She did wonder though about the species that rolled right past her usually, *the ones she'd nick-named the "ball-birds."*

They had the usual feathered body and head and wings even—bright yellow in color but there was a hint or a flavor of green there too. But it was this species feet that was unusual.

Instead of two gripping feet on legs, there was instead a scaled ball that was wider than it was tall. Each of the legs still protruded down from the bird's body, but at the end of same, they somehow acted like an axle that fit within that ball. As these yellow birds leaned forward, she'd learned from weeks of watching, that changed their center of gravity and that made the ball roll ahead. Or in any direction that the bird leaned. As the center of gravity for the bird changed, the ball rolled ahead or back—she noted that the birds never leaned to one side but always turned in a tight u-turn if they wanted to change their position.

Watching them eat was a real bit of fun, she thought, as they were all constantly jockeying for position to get the feeds from the robot feeders that were over against the far wall.

"Still, that's one hell of an unusual looking bird," she said to herself.

She did know that the late Duke's mother had actually gone into the Aviary, and had sat on a bench within and had hand fed these 'ball-birds' and she'd been told that they even allowed her to pet them.

She had not as yet ever seen any of them fly, actually and that was something she did look forward to seeing.

Till then, she said as she sipped her juice, and noted that the one with the big green splotch on it's back, was still looking at her, she'd just sit and enjoy her new pets...

Available in the winter of 2016!

Want to get early notice when we've got a new RIM Confederacy Series book launch?

Just drop by www.jimrudnick.ca and leave you email address and we'll let you know!

Or drop by our Face Book page at www.facebook.com/theRIMConfederacy/

Dear Reader...

If you've made it this far, you're most likely thinking that this was the best SciFi you've ever read or maybe not.

Maybe Tanner Scott wasn't your cup of tea?

Or you hate the Baroness and her scheming ways?

Or does the Caliph look like an upcoming tyrant?

So I'd like to ask you for a favor?

Would you mind taking a few minutes to write a review for me please?

And I'm talking honest too! Nothing makes us writers get better than book reviews!

Your comments help others know what to expect when they're looking for a great SciFi read...

And thanks once again, I'm looking forward to reading your comments!

The RIM Confederacy: Inwards Bound

Jim Rudnick
2016